PAULINE'S PERILS OF PERPLEXITY

A CAMPY COMEDY

LS Wagen

Wagen-Load Productions   Mesa, AZ 85205

PAULINE'S PERILS OF PERPLEXITY
A Campy Comedy
Published by

Wagen-Load Productions
Mesa, AZ 85205

Copyright © 2015 LS Wagen
Copyright © 2012
Revised Electronic Edition
Cover Illustration by BB Graphics

ISBN: 0-9652530-4-X

Table of Contents

Table of Contents Continued

DEDICATION

This novella is dedicated to my late parents Anna Marie, and Melvin James Bierwagen, who always believed in me and my writing abilities, and who always told me that I could accomplish anything that I set my mind to do.

Commit your works to the Lord, and your plans will be established. The human mind plans the way, but the Lord directs the steps. Proverbs 16:3 and 9 NRSV

CHAPTER 1
PAULINE'S LITTLE BREAK

Pauline Schmidt was at the Post Office teller window counting stamps for a customer, wondering how she got such a boring job. "Oh, well," she thought, "I should be happy I finally got a job, any job."

Pauline just graduated about five months ago, in December of 1984, at age 22, from Arizona State University with a double major a degree in Criminal Justice, and a degree in Quantitative Methods, taking classes in Psychology, Sociology, Criminal Justice, Statistics, and Programming Languages. "By now," she thought, "I should be using my studies as a police detective, or crime analyst." She started to imagine herself forecasting criminal behavior patterns in order to project budget requirements and manpower needs for some police department, somewhere.

"Why do they all want experience?" Pauline thought to herself, while counting stamps. Pauline had no police experience. "I should have never passed up that special Crime Analyst Internship Program, but I couldn't afford money for gas, and they refused to pay anything. Now it's too late." During her last two interviews with two local Phoenix Valley police departments, the police chiefs never even heard of getting a double major in Criminal Justice and Quantitative Methods. No one wanted to hire her without experience, and she couldn't get experience without someone hiring her. A Catch 22.

"Maybe, it would help, if I could decide which area of police work, I liked," she muttered to herself. Although petite, she was physically fit and agile, able to pass any police academy qualifications. The height and weight requirements for a police officer and detective were phased out in the seventies, so she didn't have to worry about that. She had imagined herself, as a great detective equaling Sherlock Holmes. Sometimes, she saw herself as a police chief. However, she had a hard time imagining herself shooting anybody, so she leaned toward police administration. That's why she got a job at the Post Office. She thought she could work her way up to Postal Inspector. "After all," she mused, "Mail fraud isn't that dangerous." "Who would have to shoot anybody?" she asked herself.

Pauline hated her blue postal employee uniform, with a passion, even if the color matched her eyes. Individualistic, she liked to select her own clothes, clothing in vibrant passionate colors. Every day, she thought, "Blue again, I hate blue."

Pauline got a job in a Post Office located near Arizona State University, in the Phoenix valley. She worked in San Xavier and lived at home with her parents, since she could not afford to be on her own. She had commuted to the university, and graduated from her college with honors. She had been a full time student, and today, as always, was trying not to daydream, in order to become accumulated to the world of work.

As Pauline was counting stamps for yet another customer, she flipped her black hair. She was thinking of tonight. Every Monday during the spring, she played on the San Xavier Parks and Recreation woman's softball team. This league was organized by the local city government. Although petite, thin, and lacking muscle, Pauline was an outstanding player. She also hated the spiffy "blue" uniforms, which said Bob's Bar and Grill, the sponsor, on the back. Pauline was convinced that it was her terrible fate to be always surrounded by blue.

Although Pauline's bubbly personality enabled her to get along with everybody, she didn't consider herself popular. In high school, she didn't have many friends among her fellow women's track team members, because she kept by herself, a lot. However, when she made a friend, she made a friend for life. Pauline had a lot of things going for her, but she considered herself a failure. "I'm a failure," she thought to herself dejectedly, while counting her stamps for yet another customer. "I'm always a failure. I'm not Police Chief, yet, and I don't have a current boyfriend."

Although she thought, Len Browse a distinct possibility. Len was one of her customers that always came to "her" window. In fact, "Here comes Len, now," she remarked to herself. Six feet, Len, came up to her window and said heartily, "Hello!" His short, curly red hair had been tousled from the warm, spring breeze outside. He asked her how she was, and bought a package of stamps. While remarking on the current escalating crime rate in the Valley of the Sun, Detective Len of the San Xavier Police

Department, said, "I never venture out to far alone anymore, while off duty, it just isn't safe, anymore. I just stay home."

"I stay home, too," Pauline said, confused. She wondered to herself, about just what kind of police officer couldn't protect himself. "Maybe, the gangs really are that bad," she mused silently to herself.

"You know," the detective, said, "Us, police officers have total responsibility for maintaining law and order. Without us controlling everything, there would be total chaos."

With a straight face Pauline pointed toward the picture windows that faced the street and shouted, "Look, out that window! There goes a herd of jaywalkers right now. Better go arrest them."

The detective whipped around to look, seriously expecting to see this unlawful herd of pedestrians.

"Gotcha!" Pauline exclaimed. "You're thinking that the Police and our criminal justice system can keep us safe is a myth. The only reality is that we ourselves, our own internal code of right and wrong, our collective consciousness, if you will, is what keeps us together as a society. Deep within every human soul lurks the potential of wrongdoing, the criminal mind lurking beyond the shadows. Parents are the ones controlling everything. They teach kids right from wrong. Everyone police, parents, priests, ministers, the individuals, they share responsibility. You are too hard on yourself, Detective Len; you're not 'totally responsible." Although every time there is a city election, the media claims it's the 'police's' fault. If I wasn't right, there really would be a herd of errant jay walkers out there, and all the police officers in the world, could not stop them."

"Oh, I suppose you're right," Len said dumbfounded. He admired her speech, and truly felt better about himself, and his job.

Pauline beamed. She could see by the look on his face that his self-esteem had sky rocketed, and she felt glad she could help. She really missed her college speech classes, and made up for it every chance she could.

Len departed with, "Good-by," and with his stamps.

Pauline didn't really know much about Len. Although he went to her church, she never spoke to him there. She liked to imagine that he used his stamps that he bought once a week, in investigative work, and not to write a sweetheart someplace. She deducted he was unmarried by the absence of the wedding ring.

At twelve, Pauline was relieved by Jim, and took her sack lunch out to eat at the city park bench across the street. It was a glorious Arizona, spring day, like usual. Pauline could see the Post Office from her seat in the park.

The Spanish stucco style adobe Post Office was big in order to accommodate the growing community of San Xavier, a community of about 100,000 people. The building and the customer and employee parking lots took up the whole city block.

On the way back from lunch, she checked the bulletin board to see, if there were any Postal Inspector positions available. Having only been with them one month, she was not eligible to apply for anything yet, but she checked the board anyway. No job openings.

The rest of Pauline's day went by fast. Pauline's softball team won that same night against the current Phoenix Valley Parks and Recreation champs. It was a Good Friday night game with sportsmen like conduct exhibited by both teams. Pauline caught four flies, and made three home runs. She even solved her first crime; her first crime as a working adult, anyway. Billy Green, age ten, had stolen her nephew's, Jack, age four, stick of chewing gum. She made Billy give the uneaten candy back to Jack.

As Pauline drifted off to sleep that night, she resolved to send out five hundred more copies of her resume to every police department in the country and the Virgin Islands.

She fell asleep wondering, if she will ever get her big break, or will she be solving missing candy crimes the rest of her life.

CHAPTER 2
MATTHEW'S TRAVELS

Matthew Grayson was at his desk, riffling tons of paper work, wondering how he got such a boring job. "Oh, well," he thought, "I should be happy I have a job, any job." Matt worked as a building inspector in the Facilities division of the Post Office in Washington, DC. Friday was always Matt's busiest day, as he tried to catch up on the entire week's work of paperwork, on one day.

While he was tying up loose ends, Matt wondered what his next assignment would be. Matt's mind wandered back to the time, when he was a detective for the San Francisco Police Department. He could have sworn that job was more interesting, although he knew that he had left the detectives, because he thought building inspecting would be easier. "I went back to school to study it, and everything," he thought. "Some people are never satisfied, including me," he mused silently.

At that moment, Matt's boss, Herbert Reinhardt, came in. "I have a new assignment for you, Matt. You'll like it. It involves a lot of travel, Arizona, Philadelphia, etc. It concerns our major contractor using shoddy materials, and poor construction work, while constructing the Post Office buildings. You may even have to investigate the contractor, while you're at it. You used to be a "great detective", you can do this, easy."

Matt said, "Arizona, again. I was just there."

Herb continued, "You'll be traveling all over, not just Arizona. You'll love it. Here's the list of Post Offices, their addresses, and the postmaster of each Post Office. Also here's a copy of the construction contracts, and notes, on the suspected problems of each Post Office."

Herb handed the list over to Matt while adding, "They know you are coming. Measure and inspect each building to see, if it measures up to standards agreed upon in the contract with the contractor. Oh, and you'll have to rent cars, and motels. Use the government credit card, and itemize your expenses. And don't forget the reports."

Herbert dumped a pile of reports on Matt's desk that was at least 3 inches deep.

Matt looked at this, and said, "I need more help."

"It's not in the budget. We will assign you an FBI man to work with you, once you gain more evidence. Early Monday morning, you leave for New York. Here are your tickets. Dress warm, I don't care if it is spring. I can't afford for you to get sick."

"Your concern is touching."

CHAPTER 3
PAULINE'S NEW REALITY

Pauline Schmidt was tired of solving little boy's candy crimes, and sending out tons of resumes. She decided that Saturday, was a perfect May, spring day to register for a June summer evening class in computer programming, offered at a nearby community college. She had completed courses in computers, as well as statistics, but a career in statistical analysis nowadays required knowledge of all the up and coming new computer languages. She came to this realization, after reading the classified. All the ads she had been answering lately required many courses in computer programming. She knew it would be hard fitting this class into her already busy schedule, what with work, and summer ball practice, but she was ready to try. Plus, of course, there was also church every Sunday.

Pauline was standing in line waiting to register, when she realized that this was the first time, she had registered with a community college. She had only attended a major university, ASU, since graduating from high school in 1979, at age 17. It had taken her 4 and ½ years to graduate. The community college registrar gave her a student identification card, dated June of 1985, to correspond to the beginning of the summer session.

When Pauline had no one to make speeches to, she made them to herself. She mused, "Oh, great, this student identification card, just seems to be just another thing to hang my identity on. This act of registering for a class for me is breaking my myth, and establishing a new reality. The myth that one Bachelor's degree, let alone two degrees, should take one to the top and be enough. That graduating was the end of learning, and the beginning of working. The thing is that after one graduated one wasn't supposed to have to learn anything, anymore..."

While musing about her turn of events, Pauline in a bad mood, bumped into a fellow student to be, on her way out, and Pauline didn't even say, "Excuse me." She was so upset, she didn't even notice the grocery truck, while attempting to jay walk across the street. The giant truck's brake squealed like a giant barking seal. Luckily, it stopped in time and no one was hurt. Pauline hurried off, into her light colored sea foam green sedan, which her parents had bought for her as a high school graduation present. "Just my luck," she thought as she got into her car. "Good thing Detective Len wasn't hiding behind a bush, or I would have arrested for jay walking for sure." She blushed, when she remembered her previous preaching on jay walking.

CHAPTER 4
NEW YORK, NY

Matt arrived in New York City, early Monday morning. It was late spring, but still chilly. "No wonder Herbert said to dress warm," Matt thought.

Downtown New York City was full of modern skyscrapers. Tall and skinny, the giant spindly monsters stretched heavenward. Matt was immediately homesick, for his own city's buildings, but he was determined to see New York's finest spots. After getting settled in the high-rise hotel, Matt decided to check out the Post Office. The Post Office was located downtown in an immense skyscraper. The building, made out of glass and metal, touched the sky. The glass reflected the sun, blurring the distinction, between the building and the sky.

It seemed that New Yorkers thought it was late spring and dressed accordingly. When Matt met the postmaster of the Post Office in New York, the postmaster said, "What's your problem? You look like an Eskimo." Matt proceeded to do his job. He measured the building, and inspected it. All day long, he heard snide remarks behind his back from Post Office patrons, "He looks like an Eskimo."

Matt did indeed find that the finished building did not live up to code, and he wondered why the building inspector, from the Post Office, who first inspected the building after the completed construction did not report this finding. He noted this in his report.

The next day Matt took off, as a vacation day, and toured the city. He saw the Empire State Building and bought a ticket to a Broadway play. He saw Cats, at the Winter Garden. He thought it was silly to see grown men and women dressed up as animals. He didn't enjoy the play at all. He went back to the hotel in bad sorts, because he had spent all that money on a play, he didn't enjoy and saw alone. Matt was unattached and looking, or so he claimed. Not that he had any problems attracting women, he was just particular. Matt tall, with brown almost black straight hair, won over many a lady with his charming smile. Although still strong and muscular, he didn't work out, as much, anymore, after leaving the detectives. Matt thought he didn't need to exercise like he used to. Rather handsome, he would much rather take young ladies to plays then spend his time working out. In his job, he traveled, or so he told himself, so he had no time for a relationship.

CHAPTER 5
A GIRL'S ROMANCE NOVEL

Pauline took her lunch and her contemporary romance novel to the park bench across the street from the San Xavier Post Office.

The paperback novel beckoned her. The paperback romance, yet unread, which pictured a partially unclad hunk in the embrace of his fully clad female companion, only cost thrifty Pauline 25 cents at the carport sale. Usually, Pauline would buy tons of romance novels at a time, but this was the only one at the sale that beckoned her. Perhaps it called to her because the main character was also named Pauline like herself. She turned to the page which described the beautiful scene where Matt and Pauline stopped the car at the edge of the cliff in order to admire the view of the sea.

While munching on her habitually Tuesday lunch of a baloney sandwich, she turned to the page where she read silently, "Matt's words were like sugar coated dew drops, fresh and clear, like a spring morning, words to be treasured in the secret recesses of her heart. His blue-green eyes always sparkled like the sun bouncing off the foaming sea, whenever he spoke to her. Whenever she spied her true love, Pauline's heart within her lovely bosom would beat with wide anticipation." Pauline sighed.

Then Pauline got mad, mad that real life, especially hers, was not like that. "Here take that!" she exclaimed throwing her no longer prized romance novel into the giant San Xavier's Palm Tree Park's garbage bin. Pauline ran inside the Post Office, hoping that none of the San Xavier's park's employees heard her embarrassing tirade against an inanimate object, a book.

Pauline calmed down once inside the Post Office. She didn't want her fellow employees to view anything was amiss.

In fact, Pauline's boss called her into his office. "Pauline," he said, "Good job. A little old lady wrote a commendation letter to you, which will be placed in your personnel file. Here read it." The letter said, "Your employee Pauline Schmidt is a dear. I forgot my purse, the other day, buying stamps, and Pauline ran after me a half a block with the purse to give it back to me. What a remarkable young lady!" The letter went on, "I just had to write it down, and send it to you."

Pauline beamed with pride. She was glad that all her hard work and determination was finally being recognized.

CHAPTER 6
QUICKSAND?

Matt's next stop was Albuquerque, New Mexico. He flew in there and rented a car.

When he arrived there, he told the car rental agent that he wanted a full size new '85, Ford LTD, Station Wagon, to fit his big 6' frame.

"You want a what?" said the rental agent in his snappy blue uniform.

"You heard me, a new '85 Ford LTD Station Wagon, oh, and it has to look like I'm here on vacation with my family," said Matt.

The rental agent turned his head to look around. He saw no one in the room beside Matt. "We only have Chevy's, and what do you mean by 'look like'. Where's your wife and kids, may I ask? Are they waiting for you at the airport?"

"No, they're not," replied Matt.

"Oh, what did you mean by 'look like'?" the agent asked again.

"Oh," said Matt, "I'm doing investigative work for the federal government, and I'm under cover. I'm alone, and it's a secret."

Just then a group of Japanese tourists walked in, speaking Japanese.

"Well, sir," whispered the agent. Silently waving to the tourists in the room the agent continued, "That may not be a secret anymore, considering whether or not they speak English, and understand you. But your secret is safe with me."

Then in perfect Japanese the agent yelled to the tourists, "あなたの第 2 である" which means, "Be with you in a second!"

He then turned to Matt and said, "O.K., sir we have you booked in the '85 Chevy Celebrity Wagon from today, Wednesday, May 15th, through Friday, May 17th, leaving at 3:00 p.m. We'll see you then. By the way, I need to see your driver's license." Matt handed him the license. The agent typed his license number and his birth date, October 1, 1950, into the computer.

Matt got into his rented ' 85 Chevy Celebrity Station Wagon, and continued on his way.

He checked into an Albuquerque motel for the night.

The next day, Matt headed for Small Creek, New Mexico. A favorite hunting and fishing spot for tourists. "Boy," he thought, "This sure is a quiet change from New York City!"

After renting a cabin, Matt changed into what he considered as his camping disguise, blue jeans and a blue plaid flannel shirt.

After resting for the night, he drove to the Post Office, which was off the main thoroughfare on a dirt road. It was situated near the current creek. In fact it was built on the old Small Creek bed, which existed before the creek changed its course. The Post Office was located in a mobile trailer that was permanently attached to the ground. It had a sliding glass door for the entrance, and white small wooden stairs leading to the door. He introduced himself to the elderly postmaster, Mr. Ed Brooks and his wife, Evelyn. Both Mr. Brooks and his wife, worked at the Post Office. In fact, they were its only employees, and always worked side by side.

Matt inspected the building, which fulfilled the required measurements. The problem was the ground that the building was resting on, was not evenly distributed. Over time, one end of the building had sunk two inches into the mud, looking a little like the Leaning Tower of Piazza.

"Looks, like quicksand. And no wonder built on all this clay, from the old creek bed. I bet when it rains, the creek still gathers water," Matt said to Mr. Brooks. "I wonder why the inspector that inspected this ground, before the building was put here didn't catch it. They must have done a soil analysis, and notated the ground conditions in the hydrological report. Do you have copies of the reports, Mr. Brooks?"

"Yes," replied Mr. Brooks. "I'll get them for you. It was done by a vendor out of Albuquerque. Wait outside here; I'll be back in a jiffy. They're inside in the files."

Mr. Brooks came back with the files. The report showed that there were no discrepancies in either the soil analysis report or the hydrological report; supposedly the ground was all right to build upon.

"Look, at this report, Mr. Brooks. It looks like the original material on both reports were whited out, and typed over. Do you know anything about this?"

"Heavens, no. Neither my wife, nor I know anything about that. Do we Evelyn?"

Evelyn Brooks had just emerged from the Post Office to join the gentlemen outside. "Of, course, not!" she replied.

"Well, I'll interview the firm that conducted the tests, when I get back to Albuquerque. In the meantime, I must use your phone to call my boss, to see about purchasing a new site for your Post Office." Matt went inside to use the phone.

While Matt was on the phone to his boss, the Brooks discussed him outside.

"What a nice young man, and so professional!" said Mrs. Brooks.

"I bet he has a good job," said Mr. Brooks.

"He would produce good looking children. Such a handsome lad too. Too bad he is single," said Mrs. Brooks.

"No, it's not too bad," replied Ed, "He would be just right for

Maggie." Maggie was the Brooks', twenty nine-year-old unmarried daughter.

When Matt emerged from the trailer, Mr. Brooks asked, "Want to come over for dinner tonight at our cabin? Maggie, our daughter will be there. She lives with us you know. Dinner will be at 6:00 p.m."

Somewhat taken back, Matt replied, "Yes, that would be fine. By the way, my boss is looking into getting you a new site. Oh, by the way," Matt paused, "Is there somewhere I can rent a pole and get a fishing license?"

"Yes, there is "said Mrs. Brooks," In town, at Sam's Creek's Bait and Fish Tackle Shop. It's on the main road, you can't miss it. Just head west."

"Thanks," said Matt. "At six then. My boss gave me directions to your cabin, before I left DC, in case the Post Office was closed for any reason, so I know how to find you. See you then." Matt got his six feet frame into his rental station wagon, and drove off.

"He fishes too," said Mrs. Brooks.

Matt rented a fishing pole, and bought the New Mexico state

fishing license for trout, and headed toward Small Creek, the creek from which the town was named. He got directions from the owner of the tackle shop.

He set up near a fork in the Small Creek, and started fishing for trout. As he stood on the banks fishing, he started thinking about this Maggie person. Was she pretty? Smart? What does she look like? Ed and Evelyn said nothing about her, which made him nervous. "Oh, well," he thought, "I'll only be here a short time, and maybe I'll enjoy myself. I'm kind of looking forward to it. I wish though people would stop trying to fix me up." People were always embarrassing Matt, by trying to fix him up. Matt caught zero fish that day, but he enjoyed the peaceful atmosphere that surrounded him.

At 6:00 p.m., Matt arrived at the Brooks' woodland cabin home. Matt met Maggie. He thought she was sweet and nice, but rather ordinary. She did seem to have a certain something though. She wore a lovely lavender paisley dress with a white frilly lace collar. She had shoulder length slightly curly brown hair, and puppy dog big brown eyes with gorgeous long brown lashes.

Matt didn't plan on telling Maggie the real reason for his

visit so he dressed in another disguise, a New Mexican hunting disguise, blue jeans and a red flannel shirt. He now wished that he had dressed up a little. He didn't expect Maggie and Mrs. Brooks in dresses.

Matt had a nice chicken and gravy dinner with the Brooks, and by the time the evening was over, he was just a little smitten with Maggie. Maggie seemed to hang on his every word. All he talked about was his work, and this case. What he could share of course, that wasn't secret or confidential.

After Matt mentioned that he was to be in Albuquerque tomorrow checking out the company that did the original soil analysis, and hydrological reports on the soil that the Postal trailer was resting upon, Maggie said, "I'm going to Albuquerque, myself tomorrow to visit my best friend, Lucy." Matt replied, "Why don't we have lunch together? Where shall we eat?" Mr. and Mrs. Brooks picked up their ears on that one.

"Let's eat at this great restaurant known for its Southwest cuisine, so you can tell your Washington friends, how you sampled our cooking."

"What's the name of this restaurant?" Matt asked.

"It's called Mexicali Southwest," Mrs. Brooks volunteered.

"It's at the corner of Elm and Jackrabbit Road," Ed added, pleased.

"Well," Matt said, "I'll meet you there at 12 sharp."

Shortly after this conversation, Matt said his good-byes, and thank yous, and headed back to his cabin. It was pretty late and quite dark, but he found his way back all right.

The next morning dressed in his blue uptown Washington business suite, Matt headed for Albuquerque. He drove up and down long curving mountainous roads to get there.

The minute he got into town, he stopped at a gas station and after filing up, bought an Albuquerque map. He also bought a snack, of caramel colored popcorn and peanuts. He figured no one he knew was here, and couldn't tease him this time, for buying a kid's snack. While munching on his popcorn, he read the map, and located the soil analysis place, and the restaurant where he was to meet Maggie for lunch.

When Matt arrived at Soil Analysis, Inc., he asked to speak to the president of the company. He showed the president his government badge, and told him the whole story of how he thought the report was doctored, and how he needed to compare the Post Office copy to the original. The president of Soil Analysis, Inc. helped Matt find their original test reports. It was on microfiche. He had his secretary make Matt a copy.

When Matt read the original report, he discovered that the original soil report did state that the soil was unsuitable for placing any structure on. The soil sample brought back to the lab, when enough water was added to it in order to reach its saturation point, quickly turned into quicksand. The saturated soil also failed the load/pressure test. The heavy mobile was resting on an old creek bed that still retained water during heavy rains.

"Look at this;" Matt said to the president, "It looks like the Post Office copy has been doctored. Do you think your employee did this, or our Postal building inspector?"

"Oh, no not our employee," said the President. "In fact, right now that same named employee is working in South Africa with the Peace Corps, testing the natives' soil to make sure they can build on it. Why would a man, like that, doctor anything?"

"Perhaps, you are right," said Matt, "But I'm still going to have our FBI man check out your chemist, along with our building inspector." Matt paused, "I'm going to take this report with me, and we will be in touch, if I find anything amiss concerning your on-leave employee."

"Fine," the president paused. "You do that," the president replied coldly.

Matt soon made his thank yous and good-byes, and headed toward Mexicali Southwest to meet Maggie. She was a vision of loveliness waiting for him outside the front door. This trip she was dressed in a blue paisley dress with a white lace collar. They said their hellos, and then sat down for lunch.

Matt and Maggie had a nice lunch starting with appetizers of finger sized Bean with Cheese Burritos. Next came the main entrée consisting of a Chicken Tamale Pie made with spicy chicken and corn, topped with a cornmeal crust, and for dessert, chocolate tostados, Mexican Chocolate rolled in flour tortillas, complementing the Mexican coffee. "Southwestern cuisine started with Mexican food and the people of New Mexico and Arizona Americanized it. Now, you can tell your friends what Southwestern cuisine tastes likes. "

"I suppose," replied Matt, wishing that he was eating lunch with someone less ordinary.

"Do you think..."

Matt interrupts her with, "No, I don't think we should keep in touch. Too busy."

Maggie stammers, "Well, I..., I ...never."

"It has been a nice adventure though meeting you, and all," Matt continues, "I found out about the report. Your Dad's Post Office was built on quicksand, and the original report confirms it. Your Dad's copy was doctored. I think our Post Office copy was doctored by our own building inspector, but I don't know why."

"The building isn't the only thing on quicksand; you're sinking fast," Maggie replied coldly.

However, Maggie was intrigued by the mystery, and changed the subject, "Why couldn't it have been the chemist who doctored the report, instead of the Postal employee?"

"According to the President of Soil Analysis, Inc., he couldn't have done it, too nice of a guy," replied Matt.

"What makes him nice? He took a New Mexico gal to lunch?" Maggie asked sarcastically.

"No, silly," Matt appeared oblivious to his lack of charm and the sarcasm. "He is a Peace Corp volunteer, busy saving humanity."

Although Maggie and Matt departed coldly, they both agreed that meeting each other was beneficial, as it was quite an adventure for both of them. Maggie even wished Matt luck with the investigation, and she really meant it.

CHAPTER 7
PAY ME!

Pauline got up early to pay her bills. She wanted to get them ready to mail, and off her mind. The invoices lay on the table screaming, "Pay me! Pay me!" In Pauline's mind, the exploded like a volcano erupting.

"This credit card bills is really making me angry!" Pauline said to her parents. "I just don't make enough money to cover all my bills."

"You don't have a lot of bills," her younger teenage sister said. "I have bills. I buy clothes. You have a uniform, you wear every day!"

Ignoring her sister, Pauline angrily pushed the bills into the envelopes with their corresponding checks, and licked the envelopes. She stormed off to her bedroom to get her stamps. When she got to her bedroom, she realized that she had forgotten to buy some yesterday at work, and she was out. She had two days off, and wanted them mailed today. She gathered up her purse and check book, and stormed off, "I'm going to buy some stamps."

Can't you wait until work on Monday?" they said.

"No," replied Pauline curtly, while leaving.

Pauline headed around the corner on foot to the local laundry. It was only a block away. Inside the laundry, there was a Post Office counter, which took up one corner of the room. As Pauline was arriving, the laundry attendant slammed down the door to the window of the counter. The sign posted nearby said, "Post Office window closes at 10:00 a.m., on Saturdays." Pauline beat on the door. "Open up," she cried.

"Can't," said the laundry attendant through the closed white door, "Counter closes at 10:00 a.m., and it's ten."

"Please. Don't be like that. There's no Post Office rule that says, you can't open it back up."

Oh, all right," visibly perturbed, the laundry attendant relented, and opened it back up. Curtly she sold Pauline the stamps, while Pauline licked them, put them on the envelopes, and deposited the envelopes into the Post Office box, which was right outside of the laundry.

Suddenly with that action, the bills stopped exploding, "Pay me!"

"That's a load off my mind. At least, my bills are paid, now. Never mind that my checking account reads five dollars, until I get paid on Monday. I've got to get a better job," thought Pauline.

In the afternoon, Pauline felt better she decided to go to the mall with Liza her Mexican American friend from church. Besides she thought, I can just window shop. See what the new styles are and maybe I can put together a new outfit from the clothes still hanging in my closet.

But Liza didn't want to go to the mall; she wanted to hang around the phone at home, in case some guy she likes from church might call her. He said he might call her today. When Pauline asked Liza who was this boy Liza changed the subject, and wouldn't answer.

"Oh, well," thought Pauline, "Maybe she just wants her privacy, in case things don't work out."

Pauline called up her other friend Marlene from church, and they hung out at the mall instead. Pauline's seventeen year old sister Bridget wanted to come to, but Pauline was still miffed about that "bill" comment she made earlier, and wouldn't let her come. Besides the only time Bridget seemed to want to be with her was if she could get something out of it, like a free ride to the mall. Bridget was allowed to use the family car, only if she put, and paid for the gas that went into it. Bridget's part-time receptionist job after school which was part of a school work-study program only paid minimum wage, and Bridget had quite an appetite for clothes from that mall, thus leaving little money for gas to get to that mall.

Pauline and Marlene tried on, but didn't buy nearly every dress, blouse, and pants in the mall, and spent the whole day enjoying the mall. Pauline aware that her account only had $5 left in it, of course, didn't spend a thing, not even for lunch, although she could have. She had a charge card since she was 18. Her father was a co-signer on it, and once she graduated from college, Dad let her have one on her own. She had proven responsible with it. Pauline thought, Dad would never trust Bridget with himself as a co-signer on her credit card, even when she turns 18, and graduates from high school. Pauline didn't believe in spending money that she didn't have or won't have at the end of the month when her bill came due. These bottled up emotions provided the impetus for the emotional venting that she had exhibited earlier. Pauline desperately wanted enough money to comfortably pay for all her wants, and needs by the end of the month. Just because she was frugal, and somewhat of a tomboy didn't mean she stopped wanting the same kind of pretty things that all women want. But of course, there were all those bills, car insurance, car maintenance, and other necessary items that aren't found at the mall.

When Pauline came home from the mall, she had dinner with her family, and was getting ready for bed, when Bridget came in her room wanting to see what Pauline bought at the mall. Pauline exasperated said, "You know Bridget how tight things are, I only window shopped with Marline I didn't end up buying a thing."

"What?" exclaimed Bridget, "What a waste of time; you didn't buy a thing! You have a credit card, why didn't you just charge it?"

"You know, I have to pay that money back, and I pay it at the end of them month so I don't have to pay that unreasonably high interest rate. You know what I went through this morning coming up with the dough."

"Well, I would have just charged it. Who cares if you never pay it back?"

"Haven't you ever heard of garnishments?" replied Pauline gently. It was time to stop being mad at her dear, innocent nerve wrecking sister, and time to gently educate her instead.

"Garnishments?" Bridget replied quizzingly. "What's that?"

"It's when the creditor in this case the credit card company goes to court, and gets a court order to attach your paycheck, and you are forced to pay the debt back over time. You see there really is no free lunch."

"Oh, really?

"What did you think? That there are no consequences in ignoring your bills? You know if Mom and Dad didn't pay the light bill, the utilities would eventually be turned off too."

"How did you learn all of this? Our lights have never been

turned off."

"Dad. Remember when he co-signed so I could get my first credit card when I entered college? He made Jill, and myself read all about credit, before he allowed us any credit cards. Well, he would, wouldn't he? He graduated from ASU's business school and makes a living as an accountant."

"Do you think he'll try to educate me too, when he co-signs for me?"

"Well, I never," Bridget said reacting to Pauline's tone. "

At the rate, you are spending your paycheck on clothes now, I doubt you will ever get a credit card if it was up to Dad," Pauline said factiously.

"Bridget," Pauline said, her tone more gentle, "You can't base your self-esteem on having the latest fashions, and keeping up with all your rich friends."

"You hypocrite, you were at the mall looking all day at fashions. Don't give me that! I...I... I...Did it ever occur to you, that I just like clothes. I don't worry about keeping up."

"Sure, you don't, Bridget" replied Pauline sarcastically,

knowing her sister well.

"I'm not talking to you, anymore," said Bridget curtly storming out of Pauline's room.

Pauline tired from talking, and thinking about finances vs. fashion called it a night, and went to bed, knowing that Bridget will eventually learn all this on her own anyway.

"Didn't I learn about finances the hard way, too?" thought Pauline. She recalled that her older sister Jill who graduated from ASU in Business now married with one child named Jack tried to teach her too, just like she tried to teach Bridget.

CHAPTER 8
J. EDGAR

Matt once again called the FBI man assigned to the case, late Friday night. After giving the FBI operator the code words, he was connected to the FBI man, George Kinney.

"Hi, J. Edgar Hoover," Matt said cheerfully.

"Quit calling me that," George said annoyed. "You know my real name."

"Relax, Edgar."

"What's up?" asked George, ignoring the Edgar part, hoping Matt would stop calling him that if he ignored him.

"Well, I visited Albuquerque, like I told you before when I called from Small Creek. I got the copy of the original chemist's soil report and a copy of the hydrological report from the vendor Soil Analysis. The vendor's reports showed that the ground was definitely unstable, although our copy of the report showed no abnormalities. Our copies were definitely whited out, and typed over. Grab a pen, I want you to check out the chemist."

"Gottcha, go ahead, what's his name and Social Security number?"

"Wait, one minute, his name and S.S. number is on the paperwork, I got from the Soil Analysis, Inc. company. Let me go get it."

George annoyed, grumbles to himself, "First he tells me to get a pen, then he runs off for an eternity to get the name. Why didn't the dope have that to begin with?"

"O.K., Edgar, I'm back. The chemist's name is Chris Sinkfeld. Chris with a C and his Soc. is 555-55-5555."

"O.K., I got it. I'll run a background check, and I'll also see what he's up to now. And by the way, if you keep calling me Edgar, I have a few names I could call you."

"Is there anything, else?" replied Matt.

"Yea, I'm going to run a background check on the Post Office's old building inspector, and see what he is up to now. And by the way when you go to Philly, to investigate the building, tail the contractor that built all the Post Office buildings and that sold us the building supplies, and the land in Albuquerque. As you know, his home office is in Philadelphia."

"I'm just a lowly building inspector; isn't the cloak and dagger stuff your job?"

"Yes, I know, but I'm lazy. Just do it."

"I used to be a detective for the City of San Francisco. I can handle it," Matt pridefully announced.

"Yes, I know. I did a background check on you, too. Just remember you're not a police officer anymore, so no guns or stuff. Any arresting, stuff, will be done by **me**, and me alone." "Oh, I see. I do all the work and you get all the credit. Ever heard of no guts, no glory?"

"I have guts. I'm just lazy."

"So you told me," Matt laughed, and then continued, "I'll call you, if I need you to arrest someone. But first I need evidence on the contractor, the chemist, and/or our old friend, Bill, our old building inspector."

"Did you ever meet Bill?" asked George. "He worked with you didn't he?"

"I only saw him once, briefly. Heavy set and balding on top. I would say three hundred tons, pointy nose. He quit the same time I started. His last day was my first. He never told us where he was going, after he quit us."

"Do you thing Bill changed the reports, or was it the chemist?" asked George.

"I don't know. Oh, the chemist should be easy to track. He's working for us, you know."

"Us?"

"Yea, us, you know, the U.S. government. He's a Peace Corp volunteer for outer Mongolia, or somewhere."

"Outer Mongolia?"

"Oh, really South Africa. He's testing the soil, so the Africans can build their huts, or something, safely on it."

"Their huts may be sinking in quicksand, by now," replied George.

"You know, Ed Brooks, the Post Master in Small Creek, could have changed it, or his wife Evelyn, could have, too," Matt said.

"I'll check them out too."

"OK   Well, good-bye, J. Edgar," Matt kidded.

"Good-bye," George hung up the phone laughing softly to himself.

The next day when Matt wakes up, he realizes that he has the name and business address of the contractor/land owner in Philadelphia, but he has no idea what he looks like. "How am I supposed to tail, him?" Matt asks himself.

Matt hurries to the airport, and catches the next flight to Philly. He arrives in Philadelphia, early Saturday morning.

Matt wished that it was early fall in Philly instead of spring. The leaves would have been changing to a golden yellow and crispy orange. Fall was beautiful in Philly. Matt knew this, because he had been here last fall for a building inspector convention.

Matt was a history buff, and was excited to be in the nation's old capitol. He thought the buildings, here, were different, more distinct, then his own office building at home. Matt worked in a modern looking building with streetlights that looked like popcorn, popcorn popping up on the sidewalks outside illuminating the walkways. He thought to himself, "Just think, Thomas Jefferson, John Adams, and Thomas Paine, once walked these same streets of Philadelphia. Ben Franklin walked here too, as the first Postmaster General under the Continental Congress."

After checking into his high-rise hotel in the middle of downtown Philadelphia, Matt walks over to the Post Office. He had an appointment with the Postmaster. He was surprised to find that the Post Office was open on Saturday, for some sort of promotion. Betsy Ross, or an actress dressed up like a Betsy Ross, was outside the Post Office. She had on a white cap, and was dressed in red, white, and blue. Matt stopped to talk to her. He found out her real name was Betty Finklestein and she was a Post Office employee, who dressed up to promote the new line of historical commemorative stamps. She was handing out brochures about the stamps.

Matt said to Betty, "It is strange that the postmaster would go in for something like this, as it was so commercial for a governmental entity, and to be open on Saturday, to boot, just for this."

"Yes," this is true," replied Betty. After learning that Matt was a fellow postal employee, she added, "But our postmaster is well, a little, what you call, uh, eccentric."

Matt was going to ask the spunky, short curly haired brunette to have lunch with him, until she mentioned her husband in the passing conversation. Matt switched gears, and mentioned his appointment with Mr. Greer, and asked her, where he could find him.

She gave him directions.

As Matt was walking to the postmaster's office, he thought it was strange that Philly would have such a modern looking Post Office. It was a skyscraper, not unlike his own building. "I guessed, I had pictured a red, brick Post Office with the Liberty Bell ringing out of its bell tower."

Matt walked up to Mr. Greer's 3rd floor office, and knocked on his door. His secretary probably had Saturday off, as her desk outside in the corridor was unoccupied. He spoke with Mr. Greer, and showed him his ID. Mr. Greer had been expecting him, as Matt's boss, Herbert, had already filled him in on the fact that Matt would be re-inspecting the building. Matt thought to himself, "This postmaster was a bit squirrelly just like Betsy Ross, said."

Matt got right to work. He spot-checked the plumbing and the electrical on the 3rd floor. He measured, and checked the floor against the plans, that he had brought with him. Sure enough, the dimensions came up short, again, but the building was still "sea worthy". She wasn't sinking or anything, like Small Creek.

As Matt was leaving the Post Office, his work for the day completed, he came up short. There was Ed Brooks in Philadelphia, taking mail out of a Post Office box. According to Matt, Ed would have no reason to be taking mail out of the box. Because Ed, did not seem to notice Matt, Matt decided to tail Ed, and to check with the postmaster later to find out, who owned the box.

Matt found his heart racing, as all his adrenaline came into high gear. It was fun for him to be on the chase, again, after all those years, as a boring building inspector. "I know, I am a first rate, tailor. Got an accommodation for that, back in San Francisco," he thought to himself.

Ed was going up the busy sidewalk at a brisk pace with a

load of legal sized white envelopes tucked neatly under his arm. Matt followed ten feet behind, hiding in back of pedestrians, trees, and bushes. "I'm so good," Matt thought.

Ed crossed the street, at the light, and headed back the other direction from which he came. Matt followed behind. Mat was getting very hungry, as he was missing his lunch. "I bet that suspicious looking Ed, whited out those reports, after all," thought Matt. Visions of newspaper headlines praising Matt's resourcefulness danced in Matt's head.

Ed kept up this merry chase of going back and forth in a circle in front of the Post Office for about two hours. Finally, Ed sat down on a bench to rest. Matt hid nearby behind a bush.

Suddenly, Ed stood up, came over to Matt, and said, "You look ridiculous hiding behind a bush that only half covers you. Next time, you tail someone, choose bigger bushes."

"Hold still Ed." Matt reached into his pocket, and while taking out his little pocket camera, he took a picture of Ed.

"Just what do you think, you are doing?" screamed Ed.

"Taking your picture," Matt said, feeling a little sheepish at himself for allowing Ed to catch him tailing him.

"First, you throw over my poor Maggie. And now this, you lousy ..."

"You don't have to get, huffy," Matt said quietly.

"You don't think I had anything to do with those reports, do you? Is that why you were following me? ... I have, you know, nothing to do with that. My wife doesn't either, for that matter."

"Well, the thought did cross my mind. What are you doing way over here in Philadelphia, and what were you doing taking mail out of the Post Office box?" asked Matt.

"It's none of your business, but my wife's nephew, Rick Klein-Hopper, lives here in Philadelphia, and is recovering from a cancer operation. We're his only living relatives, so I came to take care of him, and get his mail, until we can hire full time caretakers for him. Evelyn is watching the Post Office. I came this time, because she did it last time. Rick called the postmaster, and told him that I had a key to his box. You can ask him, yourself."

"No, that won't be necessary, I believe you." Mentally, Matt made a note to himself, to call Mr. Greer later.

"Who's been watching Rick, now for the last two hours?" Matt asked suspiciously.

"The part-time nurse that I hired from the agency. You know, I want this thing solved. I have not heard peep from your boss. My Post Office is sinking deeper by the day, and no new site is in sight!"

"I'll call and check with him, tonight. But you know, I read in the file that site was purchased at the request of the contractor, because it was the only site available at the time, without exercising eminent domain, of course. It still will be hard to get a site today. I'll ask him to call you at Rick's, as soon as he knows something. What's his number?" Matt asked.

"It's area code 555,555,5555." Matt wrote the number down on his note pad. He also made a note to check out the number with directory assistance to see if a Rick Klein-Hopper actually lived there.

"By the way, Matt, Maggie's got herself, a new boyfriend.

He's a CPA for a big national Certified Public Accountant firm. He lives in Albuquerque. He's got lots of potential."

"What did you mean by new boyfriend? Maggie and I just dated once. Surely, you don't consider me an ex-boyfriend."

"I thought you had potential. And yes I did."

"Maggie, didn't think, I was her boyfriend, did she?" asked Matt.

"I don't know, didn't ask her. This one doesn't hide in bushes."

"Do you want to have lunch with me, Ed? I'm hungry," Matt said, trying to change the subject.

"Heavens, no," Ed thought to himself, "This idiot didn't even guess that I knew that he was following me all along."

"Well, I did enjoy meeting you and your family, Ed. Maggie is a great girl. We just weren't made for each other. I wish her luck with Mr. CPA, whoever, he is." Matt really meant it.

"Well," said Ed calming down, "I appreciate that. I really do need to get back to Rick. The nurses' shift is just about over."

"Well, good-bye, then," said Matt.

"Good-bye," said Ed, shaking his head slowly, and chuckling softly to himself as he leaves.

Matt headed over to the restaurant, across the street, to have lunch. Before he orders, he heads over to the pay phone. First, he checks out Rick Klein-hopper's address with directory assistance. Everything, matched up. Next, he called Rick's. He got the nurse. "Does Rick Klein-Hopper, live here? I have a vacuum cleaner, I want to sell him." Matt asked the woman on the other end of the line. "He's indisposed right now. I'm his nurse. Please don't call, anymore. He's sick," and the nurse hung up on him.

Next, he called Mr. Greer, and found out that Ed told the truth, when he said Rick called him. Mr. Greer said, he knew Rick, a long time. Rick came every day to the Post Office. He had some sort of home business, where he needed to collect his checks from the box.

Next, Matt called his boss, at home. Herbert Reinhardt was

a little upset to be called at home on Saturday. Matt told Herbert about the incongruities found in Philly, and asked him to check into the Rick Klein-Hopper story. He played down the chase part, because he was embarrassed, and just told him that he had bumped into Ed, in Philly, and Ed wanted to know about his new site. He gave his boss, Ed's nephew's phone number. Herbert said that the Rick story sounded suspicious, and promised he would look into it, and into a new site for the New Mexico office, on Monday.

Matt ate his lunch, and then went back to the hotel room, for a long, long, nap. He was very tired, from following Ed around all day.

Matt had dinner in his hotel room, while watching the local news on television. He then went to bed, still tired. As he drifted off to slumber land, Matt noticed through the sleepy fog that the newscaster delivered his block of bad news with a sweet smile, as if to say, "Watch me. It's fun; ignore the bad news."

Matt woke up early the next morning, in order to attend church services early as was his custom at home. After church, Matt decided to eat brunch in a restaurant on the outskirts of the city, so he could soak up some local color. Matt decided to eat lunch in a restaurant on the outskirts of the city, so he could soak up some local color. Ravenous with hunger, he ordered steak, potatoes, and veggies, along with a soda pop. Matt's soda pop sizzled and popped like bacon on a hot stove. Always the undercover detective, he drank the soda pop quickly, so it wouldn't make all that noise.

While drinking in the scenery, he couldn't believe his eyes. Bill Graham, the old building inspector walked in, and took a seat in the corner, next to a gentleman in a blue, business suit. Matt hid behind a menu, so Bill wouldn't notice him.

Matt's hearing ability was as good as his eating skills, and he could hear every word. Bill was talking to, yes, was it, the Post Office's original building contractor, Joe Bloom, from XYZ, Inc. Matt didn't recognize Joe, never having met him, but he picked this up from the conversation. At least Matt knew now who he should have been tailing. He finally learned what Joe looked like. Mr. Bloom was the head of a very large national construction, and real estate development firm. He seemed like an authoritative, but personable sort. He wore his position like a cloth. A robe of authority easily put on and taken off.

Joe Bloom was attempting to blend in with the relaxed atmosphere of the restaurant. He was loosening his tie, and taking off his jacket.

Matt quietly paid his check, so he was ready to follow them, when they left.

The two men did not say anything very revealing. When they left they split up, into separate cars. Matt decided to follow Joe, instead of Bill. Bill would probably recognized Matt, eventually. Matt in his station wagon, carefully followed behind Joe's red Jaguar.

He followed Joe ninety miles outside the city of Philadelphia, into the countryside town of Greenwood, Pa. Joe stopped at a general store that actually looked like a Philadelphia building should look like, a red brick building with a bell and bell tower, on top.

Matt followed him inside the store. In the corner of the store, there was a Post Office. Joe opened a Post Office box, and removed some beige legal sized envelopes.

Matt hid behind the soda pop display, to watch. After Joe left, Matt stayed behind to talk to the postmaster, slash, general store owner. Matt debated following Joe further, but he gave up that idea, because his rental car was almost out of gas. He thought, "Yes, even detectives run out of gas. Only in the books, and in the movies, do the police never run out of gas at inopportune times. The fictitious detectives' cars never have to be fueled, even bumbling detectives like "Columbo," never run out of gas. If the car companies knew the secret of these miraculous cars, they would make a mint. But this is real life. I better go talk to the postmaster here."

Matt talked to the grocery owner, and identified himself. He showed him, his ID and told him the basics of the case. He got the PO number of Mr. Bloom's box, and asked the postmaster to keep track of Joe's comings and goings. He asked him to keep it quiet. Matt asked him if he could use his phone.

Matt looked up Mr. Blooms' home address. He already had his work address. Matt thought to himself, "It's Sunday, Joe

Bloom should be at home. Another unmovie detective type thing to do, using phone books as detective tools, how mundane, not real exciting." By using his calling card, Matt attempted to reach his FBI agent, but he was off on Sunday. Matt left a message that he would call him tomorrow, after arriving in Phoenix.

Later that afternoon, and with a full tank of gas, Matt drove by Mr. Bloom's house. He parked outside across the street, all afternoon, but never saw Bloom's Jaguar. Mr. Bloom's station wagon was home, and his two young children were playing out front in the front lawn. Joe lived on a quiet middle class residential street. Well, Matt thought, if he's stealing from us, the money isn't being spent on his house.

Matt finally gave up around 5 p.m.., stopped for a bite, and went back to his hotel room, and went to bed. He was to get up early tomorrow for the flight to Phoenix.

CHAPTER 9
WINDOW SHOPPING

Bob's Bar and Grill had a Saturday night game. Pauline was excited all day over the game. She even forgot about her money problems that she had earlier in the day.

And she had a plan. One of the San Xavier's police officer's wives was on her team. Maybe, she could get to know her better, and that could be her in, into the department.

When Pauline was in the dugout, getting ready to practice, Officer John Branson, came rushing up behind the dug out to talk to his wife. Officer John was in plain clothes, as he was off duty. "Marilyn!" he said excitedly, rushed, "Guess what happened? I left my wallet on the car seat, and locked all the doors. I went back to get it and the door window was broken and my wallet is gone!"

"What!" Marilyn exclaimed, obviously annoyed,

"You think because you are an officer of the law, you are exempt from this kind of stuff! You left it out in plain view! Really!" She calmed down, "Let's go home right now, and take our broken car with us. We'll have to get it fixed before I can drive it."

Marilyn turned to Pauline, "Tell the coach, I had to leave. Tell the coach, you can have my spot, as shortstop. You don't belong in center, anyway."

Pauline thoroughly mystified thought, "What was he doing leaving a wallet out like that? He really does think he is exempt." She laughs softly to herself and thinks, "Well, I got my break, anyway, kind of. At least, I'm playing shortstop, for one game anyway."

As she was walking across the field to talk to the coach, who was over by third coaching third base, she thought, "Maybe, I don't want to work for this San Xavier department, after all, with employees like that."

She told her coach the whole story including what she had thought about the San Xavier police department. Coach said, "No, you sure don't want to work for that crazy City. Yes, you can play shortstop for one game. Do you know what I heard yesterday?" The coach never could keep a secret.

"No, what?" asked Pauline eagerly.

"I heard from my cousin the building inspector, that there were rumors that an ol' building inspector named Bill Graham, was taking kickbacks from some ol' contractor who built buildings around here, some guy in Philadelphia. They couldn't prove it, so they fired him on some trumped up sexual harassment charge. I hear they baited him. After that ol' Bill, dropped out of sight. Was never seen from again."

"Oh, that's interesting," Pauline replied. She thought, "Oh, great a genuine mystery. I love mysteries. Especially, ones I could solve. Maybe San Xavier would not be such a bad place to work after all."

Pauline was wonderful as shortstop. They won the game, twenty three to eleven. They had never done that well, before. Pauline knew it was all because of her. Maybe, Marilyn would quit the team, to keep track of her husband and his wallet, and she could keep the spot, permanently.

The next day, Pauline, got up early to go to Mass. Her young adult group from church was going to go after Mass, to feed the homeless, at the shelter. She wondered if she should really be doing this.

In the first place, it was Sunday, and she wasn't really keeping the Lord's Day as a day of rest. But then she thought, the Lord did good things on Sunday, like cure the sick, so it was O.K. Another problem was that they really didn't have health license to serve food yet, at the new shelter, and they were technically breaking the law.

"Would that affect my chances to become Police Chief of San Xavier, some day? Breaking the law," she wondered. She decided to do it anyway, as nobody these days seemed too concerned about feeding the poor. And Pauline herself was poor. She told herself, "If Mom and Dad weren't taking care of me, I would be among them, on my salary."

She did, however, make sure everything was taken care of, sanitary, and otherwise. Before the game yesterday, she personally bought hairnets, for everybody. She even bought them for the guys. And the men in her group had short hair. She still felt guilty, but she knew that the health license was coming in soon, as the shelter had applied for it. Besides, her group had made the newspapers. The newest issue in town. An example of the good intentions v.

lack of food service license controversy. If the Police wanted to arrest them, they would have done it, by now. "Now, if only I can solve some big crime, and make the paper for that, I could easily get a police job."

The air conditioner was broken again at the shelter, and it was hot! Pauline's passion for helping the homeless gave way to her sense of smell and the heat. She felt dizzy. Her clients, as Pauline called the homeless, seemed concerned over her welfare.

The homeless told her about how they got into that situation. Most of them had really good jobs in the past. Some of them even had doctorate degrees. Some of them like Pauline, had been living on a small salary from paycheck to paycheck, but they had no relatives to help them. When they lost their jobs, and unemployment ran out, they were on the streets. The eighties were hard times; they were in a deep recession.

The ceramic counter, which divided the young adult group, was only a physical barrier, not an emotional one for Pauline. There was no genuine separation; they all shared a common humanity, each one with his or her own life story. "I could be one of them, and they could be one of me," she thought.

Just then one of Pauline's clients had an epileptic seizure. His wife said that they couldn't afford the medicine, and he had been off of it too long. The shelter's director called the police, and the paramedics. "Oh, no," Pauline thought, "I'll be arrested for health violations, for sure."

The police and fire personnel came, and took the patient off to the county hospital. They couldn't care less, that the group was feeding her clients lunch. They didn't even acknowledge the group's existence with a "Hello."

"Well, what do you know about that!" said Pauline to her fellow workers, "Not even a 'Hello,' and we thought we would be arrested."

After lunch, the men and the women split up. The men exclaimed that they were through hanging around women that made them do unmanly stuff, like wear hairnets. Pauline felt bad, and totally unfeminine, for not coaxing the male ego. But she knew she did the right thing.

The young ladies of the group ended up eating lunch at the

giant San Xavier shopping mall. They were too sick of smelling the processed ham Spam sandwiches that they made for the poor, to end up eating lunch with their clients. They decided on serving that menu, because it was nutritious and cheap. They had paid for this lunch out of the groups' common fund.

Never again would Spam be on her menu. "I hope they don't think, that we think we are too good to eat lunch with them. It's just after smelling that stuff all day. I felt like puking," Pauline said over lunch to her girlfriends. It wasn't just the Spam; it was the Spam order mixed in with body order caused by the homeless not having everyday access to bathing facilities.

Pauline's friends, Liza, replied, "Never mind that, you chased away all the guys, which was the purpose of this outing. You said your goal this year was to 'catch some guy', but you'll never catch any by the way you're going. And we won't either. Making the guys wear hair nets, really!"

"Oh, Liza," Jolene said, "You shouldn't want a guy just because he's a hunk, or the rest of the world thinks so. Or because it's your goal, or you said you could 'catch him'. Leave her alone."

Marlene replied, "I don't know about that, I want a boyfriend, you know. My Mom says I'm nothing without a husband and two point 5 children. All the popular girls at college have boyfriends, you know. I want a boyfriend to be 'in'." "Two and half children" was the running joke among the group. The newspaper had reported that the average '80's family had two and a half children. Nobody knew how to divide up a child.

Pauline pipes up, "Oh, Marlene, your Mom, is getting old. She's older than mine. She is afraid, she'll die without being a Grandma, and is just trying to hurry you along."

Jolene added, "I bet the guys right now, are having the same conversation. I think Tom kind of likes you, Pauline. If you changed like Liza wants, he wouldn't be attracted to you anymore. Don't try to change your personality to be what you think he wants. If you do, you probably wouldn't like Tom, anymore, either."

Marlene added, "Yea, I bet Tom, right now is regretting that remark he made about those hair nets. I know he likes you, and you like him. I can tell. Remember when we ran into him at the mall one Saturday. He was making eyes at you..."

Pauline interrupting said, "Just shut up you all! Let's leave, and go shopping."

"Can't," said Marlene, "All the shops close early on Sunday."

"Well, it's only two," Pauline replied, "We can hit some stores, and then we can window shop for a while, and then go across the street, right before they close the mall doors, and see a movie."

"All right," replied Marlene, "I thought you were the one who said we shouldn't do anything on Sunday, except pray."

"I'm making an exception," Pauline replied trying to divert attention from her boyfriend-less position in life, so upset was she, with her friends' behavior.

The young ladies wandered around the mall and oohed and aahed over all the new shoes, and dresses in the windows. On their way out they passed by a little Post Office that was located inside the mall. All it had was basically a small room with a counter, where they sold stamps and received outgoing mail. It was dark and closed.

"There's your old friend," Liza said.

"Whose old friend?" Pauline asked.

"Yours.' The Post Office. Isn't your career that you tell us about all the time, your friend? That's going to be all that keeps you warm at night."

"Oh, grow up. That's not my old friend! Buildings aren't my friends. And if you don't behave Liza, you won't be either," Pauline snapped.

CHAPTER 10
THE PRO

After landing at Phoenix's Sky Harbor International Airport, Matt decided to stop at an airport restaurant for a Monday brunch. He hadn't eaten yet, as he had to leave as early as possible in order not to miss his plane out of Philly. A cute petite peppy blond served him his brunch of eggs, ham, and soup. As he was eating, he thought about his last visit here. He liked it here. The sun was always shinning, the birds were always singing, and no boss was barking orders in his ear. If he were to move anywhere else, it would be here to Phoenix.

Although the crime rate would hardly be a step up, Washington DC let the nation, in crime; Phoenix was third. Phoenix; however, had less violent crime, most of the crime was white collar. "The kind of crime, he was chasing," thought Matt. After all construction fraud was white-collar crime, rarely violent. Phoenix had its share of gang violence; however, and car thefts.

After renting this '85 Ford LTD Station Wagon from the nice

fellows in the snappy blue uniforms, he got settled in his hotel in San Xavier. The hotel was an historical landmark, built in the Southwest style. He paid for the room with his governmental credit card, knowing he would get a lecture from his boss in over indulgence. His boss, Matt knew, would have wanted him to stay in some rat infested budget motel.

"I must call J. Edgar," Matt thought, "Catch that FBI man up-to-date." Matt dialed the FBI man, George Kinney, from his hotel room. After being passed through, he reached George.

"Hi. J. Edgar."

"Oh, it's you again," George replies. George continues, "Before, you tell me what's up, let me tell you what I found out. I checked out the chemist, and yes, he is on sabbatical with Soil Analysis, Inc., with the Peace Corp in Africa. He checks out O.K. And then I checked out Ed and Evelyn Brooks. They had a thorough background check done on them, right after World War II ended in 1945, in their younger days, when they were both applying for jobs at the

71

Post Office. But I ran another check on them. They checked out fine."

George continues, "The first background check was very thorough. Since they both were of German descent, the government checked them out thoroughly, having just fought a World War II with Germany, and all. The government even baited them. Sent Ed fake Communist recruiting brochures, which listed meeting times and dates, then followed Ed and Evelyn around town to see if they would show up at one of these meetings. It was the McCarthy era of the '50's, and all, you know."

"Oh," said Matt. "Brooks doesn't sound German to me?"

"It isn't," George replied. "Ed and Evelyn legally changed their name after they were married from Krause to Brooks. After this incident, I guess they were tired of being tagged."

"Do go on," replied Matt.

"Well, it seems that Ed and Evelyn led the FBI agent on a merry goose chase all over town, bar hopping from one bar to another. Ed never showed up at the pretend meeting. In fact sometime right before the last bar closed, he turned on his heels, and said to the FBI man, 'I know who you are. You can have this stupid job, if you want. Just because my great grandparents came from Germany, doesn't mean I am a commie. You got some nerve following me around all night! Aren't US citizens deserving of some privacy! You can bait me all you want; I don't bite. And stop tailing me and my fiancée!'" According to the report, Evelyn was in the ladies' room during this conversation. The FBI man, at this point, just laughed, and left. Ed and Evelyn Brooks checked out all right, and got their jobs.

After getting married, the pair left Montana, and transferred to Small Creek, where they became postmaster and postmistress, you might say. In Small Creek, they had their daughter Maggie. Even though they married at a young age, they had Maggie, late in life, their only child. They were there helping to set up the new Post Office in Small Creek, at the time, our ol' friend Bill, the building inspector, was O.K.'ing the land for the Post Office in Small Creek. The Brooks check out alright."

"Oh," said Matt quietly, blushing. He was never going to

anyone about the merry chase Ed, led him on, nor was he going to tell George about Ed's nephew in Philly, Rick Klein-Hopper. Matt just hoped that his boss wouldn't say anything about this embarrassing incident to George.

"Oh, and Matt," George said.

"Yes, go on," said Matt.

"I checked out the current whereabouts of Bill Graham, the inspector. After leaving the Post Office, Bill worked for six months, as an inspector in Greenwood, Pa., and then worked for a year in San Xavier, for the City of San Xavier, still in government. After he left San Xavier, he dropped out of sight. I checked his social security number; there has been no activity for at least a year."

"Really," Matt continued, "I'm in San Xavier now checking on the building. I can do some investigating."

"So, Matt, what did you come up with in Philadelphia?"

"Well, the electrical and plumbing is all right in Philly. The dimensions on the building came up short. I did follow our friend the contractor. Joe Bloom was having dinner with, guess who, Bill Graham. I followed Joe. Joe stopped at a

General Store, slash, Post Office in Greenwood, Pennsylvania, just outside of Philly."

"Really! What luck! Greenwood is where Bill worked for a time, for the city's inspection department. What did you learn?"

"Well, Joe has a box there. I asked the owner to watch his comings and goings. I told him the basics of the case. Maybe, you can get a warrant to see what's in the box, box number 99. The postmaster's number in Greenwood is 555, 555,5555. His name is Mike Brown."

"I thought, Matt that you were a professional!"

"What?" said Matt questioningly.

"Do you tell everyone you meet about the case? Do you want to tip everyone off!" George exclaimed.

"I'm sorry. I didn't think of that," Matt replied sheepishly.

For sure, now Matt wasn't going to tell George about Ed's game of cat and mouse.

"Well, as long as the cat's out of the bag, I'm getting a warrant for that Post Office box. Is there anything else, you learned?" George asked.

"No," said Matt hurriedly. "I got to go. Good-bye."

"Good-bye," said George, wondering why Matt finally stopped calling him J. Edgar, and why all of a sudden long-winded Matt wanted to get off the phone.

Matt, anxious to forget about work for a while, after making a fool out of himself, decided to take the rest of the day off as a vacation day, and go sightseeing.

He went to the Heard Museum in Phoenix, where he saw the collection of Hopi Kachina dolls. The Hopi's make dolls in the image of their gods. In fact, the statues become the gods. Matt thought the coyote looking doll, reminded him of Bill, because of Bill's pointy nose.

Matt also enjoyed the Heard's African antique shrunken head collection. He told the tour guide off handedly, "I know a chemist. Right now, he is probably doing this shrunken head thing in Africa, right now." The museum tour guide looked at him strangely.

After lunch at a posh downtime Phoenix restaurant, which Matt charged on his government's credit card, he took off for Scottsdale's 5th Avenue shops, expensive shops full of Western doodads for the tourists, and fancy Western art. Matt thought, "I'm leaving a trail of credit invoices all over town, if someone wanted to follow me." He did, however, buy his Native American straw basket and his postcards with his own credit card. "He would never misuse his governmental credit card," he told himself.

Into the early evening, Matt had dinner in the hotel's restaurant. He ordered Southwest cuisine, again, kind of, developing a preference for it. "I could stay here, in Arizona, forever," he thought.

He went to bed early, exhausted from all his sightseeing. "I didn't even run out of gas today. What a wonderful day, sightseeing," Matt dreamingly thought drifting off to sleep.

CHAPTER 11
THE MEETING

Very late Monday night around midnight, Pauline called the San Xavier City recorded job hotline. She called them this late, because she couldn't get in any other time. The line was always busy, with everyone looking for work. Pauline was disappointed as the only job offered was a temporary clerk slash typist position in the building inspection department.

Tuesday morning she overslept, but she did make it in on time. At work Pauline's boss, the postmaster, Mr. Mead, was talking to some good-looking guy with a glowing pink salmon colored sunburn in the hallway. She couldn't help, but overhear their conversation, as Pauline's boss always talked 10 decibels higher than everyone else, and never acted like any of his employees even existed. He never seemed to worry about being overheard.

Pauline's ears picked up, as she heard the name Bill Graham, building inspector. She remembered Sam, her coach, telling her how, he was suspected of fraud and bribery at the City of San Xavier. "Now that is a mystery," she thought.

Apparently from the loud conversation, Pauline gathered that Matt, the good looking muscular new Postal building inspector, suspected Bill Graham, the old Postal building inspector of taking kickbacks from a contractor out of Philadelphia. "My goodness!" Pauline thought, "This same inspector that had worked for us, worked once for San Xavier. I wonder if I should tell my boss, what I know?"

She heard Matt go on as to how their own San Xavier Post Office was built with shoddy material. Apparently, the insulation was below code, which was driving up San Xavier's Post Office's utility bills to a point beyond belief. "I'll never get my raise," thought Pauline, "If all the budgetary money is going to pay the sky high summer utility bills, maybe, I should say something about the inspector?"

Just then Matt said sheepishly, "Maybe we should talk about this privately in your office. We're getting kind of loud out here." They retired into the postmaster's office behind closed doors.

At this point, Pauline was relieved for lunch. She took one of her paperbacks, and her sack lunch across the street to the park bench. However, she was too keyed up to eat or to read her romance novel. "Wow, my first real mystery!" she said to herself.

Just then, Matt, complete with his own sack lunch walked across the street, and sat beside Pauline. "Hi," said Matt. "My name is Matt Grayson. I'm a building inspector from headquarters, traveling on business."

"Hi. I'm Pauline Schmidt, lowly Arizona Postal clerk," Pauline nervously replied.

"Can I join you for lunch? I brought my own sack lunch especially made for me by the hotel," Matt asked.

"Sure," said Pauline, her heart beating faster by the minute due to handsome Matt's close proximity. Catching her breath Pauline decided to make the most of God given opportunity.

"I may be a lowly Postal Clerk employee right now, but I studied Criminal Justice in school, and I'm going to be a great detective someday."

"Really," replied Matt impressively, "I used to be a detective for the San Francisco police, got tired of it, and now I'm building inspector for the Post Office."

"You got tired of it!" exclaimed Pauline. "You must miss it. That must have been why they put you on the building inspection kickback case. I couldn't help, but overhear the whole story. You guys were really loud in the hallway."

"Yea, I know, couldn't keep Mr. Mead, quiet," Matt replied. Continuing, "Please keep it under your hat."

"I can do better than that. I can help." Pauline then proceeded to tell Matt about the rumor, she heard from Coach Sam, about Bill, and San Xavier, and the kickbacks, and the phony sexual harassment charge.

"Thanks for the information. Yes, he did drop out of sight. In 1979, at the building inspection convention in Philadelphia, I never saw Bill, and I expected to. If only I could get some physical evidence, like kickback records, or such."

Pauline's lightning bolt brain kicked in and an idea emerged, "I can help! There's a job opening for a temporary typist in the building inspection division. If I could get a leave of absence somehow, and keep my Post Office medical benefits, and seniority, and work for San Xavier at the same time, I could uncover something."

Matt replied, "That's a great idea! I know a FBI man, who could pull some strings. Get you hired post haste, instead of waiting three weeks, for a background check. I'm sure we could maintain your status with the Post Office. Legally, you would be an employee of San Xavier, and could go through their records, without a search warrant."

Pauline exclaimed, "That would be great! I want to keep my seniority here in case I decide to become a Postal Inspector, instead. Besides, being a temporary, permanently, doesn't pay too well."

Matt stood up. "Let's get started. We'll go talk to your boss right now. I'll call my boss, and the FBI man. I can be your contact. I can pretend to be your boyfriend, and meet you for lunch every day. Let's go."

Pauline gazed lovingly at her new hero and boyfriend, as they walked to the office together. A boyfriend who coincidently like the character in her new book was also named Matt.

On Wednesday morning, Pauline stopped by the San Xavier's tiny, but growing Personnel office, to apply for the temporary position. She took the application blank from the Personnel Clerk, Miss Gail Bernside. Miss Bernside told her, "Here, fill this out. After you're done, we will give you a grammar and filing test, plus a typing, word processing, and data processing test. It should take about three weeks, before you hear anything. Job posting closes today, so you got in under the wire."

Pauline took her application blank to a corner of the room, and quietly made it out. While working on it a big burly portly man rushes in madly waving an application blank and demands to see Miss Bernside. "Miss Bernside, I have my application blank done for the Civil Engineer's position. I demand to be interviewed this minute!"

"Mr. Black, you know I told you this position closes

today on May 15th, and that it takes one week to go through the material, and three weeks to run background checks on the top five. You won't get an interview for weeks, that is, if you make the top five," replied Gail Bernside in a dignified manner.

"I demand to be seen!" huffed and puffed a roly-poly Mr. Black. He raged, "I am a busy man, and my time is very important!"

"But Mr. Black, do you have a job to get back to?" asked Miss Bernside.

"No, I'm unemployed right now. I want to be interviewed this minute. Go get the head engineer right now!" he reiterated.

"I don't understand, if you're not employed right now, what do you have to do that's so important?" Miss Bernside asked.

"Well, I never," Mr. Black sputtered. Pontificating, he continued, "You're just a lowly Personnel Clerk. What do **you** know about engineering? Go get the head engineer!"

Miss Bernside's voice never wavered, although Pauline could tell other things by the look on her face.

"The head engineer is otherwise engaged. He will make his

own appointments in four weeks. You'll just have to wait until then."

Mr. Black then threw his application blank on Miss Bernside's desk, and stomped out without saying a word.

At this point, Pauline had completed her application, and walked over to Miss Bernside, to turn it in.

"Gail, I couldn't help, but overhear, it being a small room. No one deserves to be treated like that. I could tell by the look on your face that it got to you. Yelling, at you isn't going to get him the job. No wonder that blowhard is unemployed, as he is lacking in social skills. It doesn't matter what your position is here, everyone should be treated with human dignity."

"Oh, what a peach, you are. How did you know my name was Gail?" she chuckled.

"It's on your name tag. Oh, I'm sorry. I shouldn't call you by your first name, but I didn't know if it was Miss, or Mrs., or Ms., or what."

"Oh, Gail is fine. Call me Gail."

"I bet you have something to say, about him getting hired. I'm sure the Chief Engineer, will ask you about his social skills."

"Yes, his social skills were definitely lacking. Are you an employee, yet?" kidded Ms. Bernside.

"No, Ms. Bernside, you know I came in here to apply for the temporary position, in the Building Inspection office. I hope to work my way up to Police Officer, someday. Do you like working here? I mean, most of the time; not on days like this when people yell at you."

"Not an employee, yet. Well, will have to see what we can do about that situation. And yes, I like working here a lot. We get quite a few of Mr. Black's, in here, though."

"Well, I want to be an employee here. People are nice, here. What do I do next?"

"Well, let's have you take the tests that I mentioned earlier, and then, I'll interview you. I'm in charge of making the hiring decisions, with the temporaries."

Pauline aced all her written tests. She typed sixty words per minute on the typing test, and did as well on the word processing program. She excelled at the data processing test as well.

"So, Pauline, you did very well, on all your tests. For sure, I'm going to make sure you get employed here somehow, someway. I see by your application, that you went to college, and just left the Post Office." Gail was already starting to call Pauline, by her first name, instead of Miss Schmidt.

"Gail, don't you want to ask me any questions? You haven't asked me one question?"

"Oh, Pauline, I already know, all I need to know about you. Just have to run a background check. Check back with us in three weeks."

"Oh, O.K.," said Pauline, taking her leave. "Apparently," though Pauline as she left, "the FBI hadn't contacted the Personnel office, yet. Wow, I'm getting this job, on my own!"

Pauline left the San Xavier's Personnel office, and drove the two blocks over to the Post Office. She changed into her uniform, in the ladies' room. After exiting the ladies' room,

Mr. Mead, the postmaster called her into his office, apparently no more hallway conversations. He shut the door, and said, "The FBI man, George Kinney, is going to contact the San Xavier's Personnel office later today, and is going to fax them, a copy of your background check that you had one month ago, when you joined us at the Post Office. He's going to explain things, and make sure you are employed, posthaste. I'm glad that you went over there earlier this morning to apply. By the way, Matt, your contact, is moving out of his hotel room, and in with me, and my wife, and three kids, in the guest bedroom, the one that is reserved for my mother-in-law visits. Grandma will just have to wait."

Mr. Mead continued, "Can't have him spending all the Post Office's money on fancy hotel rooms, now, that we have to spend tons of tax payer money on making Post Office building renovations, to get them up to code. Besides, this gives him a cover. We're going to tell, people, that your new boyfriend, is my nephew visiting here from Washington DC."

"Yes, that is good," Pauline said, "We should try to keep it as close to the truth as possible, so we don't get caught lying. If the San Xavier police stop him for speeding in his rented station wagon, that I saw him get into in the parking lot, they'll see that he has a Washington DC driver's license. By the way does any of the San Xavier Police force know about this undercover operation?"

"No, Pauline," Mr. Mead seemed definite on that, "And we're going to keep it that way. Only the Personnel office, will know. If our friend Bill, was taking kickbacks, we want to know, why the Police didn't do anything."

Pauline's face fell, along with all of her hopes in impressing the San Xavier's Police department. "Well," she said, "They did get him fired on a trumped up sexual harassment charge, or that's the rumor. So they did do something."

"Yes, I know that. Pauline, you told me that before. Well, back to work."

"I don't want my parents to know, or my friends, about me being undercover. They think I'm spending my days at the Post Office. The San Xavier's office is not going to call my home, to tell me when to start?"

"No, they'll call here later today. I told the FBI man that your parents must not know. No one must know. The rest of the employees, think you couldn't cut it at the Post Office, and they have been told you're taking a job elsewhere."

"Are you sure that the Post Office, won't make up the difference in salary from the San Xavier job, and this one? I can't pay my car insurance bill, unless I borrow money from Mom and Dad, and then they'll wonder what I spent it on, and why I needed it to begin with? And they will wonder how I became so irresponsible. " Pauline hated looking irresponsible.

"No, Pauline. Can't do that. We did keep your seniority and benefit package."

"Well, I hope this is not a long involved ordeal. I start summer classes in June. But I guess it's worth it. Maybe, it'll help me move up to Postal Inspector."

"Well, Pauline, I'll put in a good word for you, as a swell sport, if a Postal Inspection position ever opens up."

"Oh, uh, thank you Mr. Mead."

CHAPTER 13
AUNTIE!!

Wednesday, as Matt was driving his rental to the airport, he kept replacing the words "April Love" in the song on the radio "April Love," with the words, "May Love." "Better in keeping with my role as 'boyfriend, and after all it is May,'" he thought to himself. Matt loved to sing along with the oldies on the radio. Matt loved the Phoenix oldie station. It played all his favorites.

He turned into the car rental lot, next to the airport, and went inside to talk to the agents in his best loved, bright, snappy, blue uniforms. "I love blue. Those uniforms remind me of the Post Office uniforms," thought Matt.

"Hi, there," Matt says to the familiar agent. "Remember me? I'm not a family man anymore. I'm just a rich boyfriend. I'm here to trade my station wagon, for a fire engine red little sports car."

"Are you playing boyfriend, or is this for real this time?" asked the agent.

"Maybe yes, or maybe no," replied Matt.

After Matt, left with his bright new 1985 shiny red sports car, the agent noticing the room was devoid of customers, said to his coworker, "He says he's a detective, but I saw his ID for the military slash government discount. It says building inspector for the Post Office on it. Technically, the Post Office is not part of the U.S. government, but I didn't want to argue with him. I gave him the discount anyway. We get all the nuts, you know. Think it's the uniforms that attract them?"

His fellow rental agent, Doreen replies, "Yea, last week a guy from Connecticut came in to rent a car. He thought he was Marshall Dillon, for sure, with his broad beamed cowboy hat, and spurs. Said he was going to Tombstone and Old Tucson, ma'am."

The agent said "Tombstone, and Old Tucson, ma'am" in an affected Texan-drawl imitating the customer, who was trying to sound "Western," and failing at it. No one in Arizona drawls. Drawls are of a Texas affectation. Nor do genuine Arizona cowboys wear spurs downtown. The agents laughed softly to themselves.

Matt, meanwhile, picked up his stuff from the fancy hotel.

He had no trouble fitting all his many suitcases in the station wagon, but had trouble stuffing them into the tiny sports car's trunk. The hotel employees watching this from a distance through the window thought it was hilarious to see Matt pouncing on the trunk to get it to close. They had all seen it before. Some of the suitcases eventually ended up in the back seat.

Matt arrived at the postmaster's house, and knocked at the door while grinning a Cheshire cat's smile.

A premature gray haired woman in her early fifty's opened the door.

"Hello, Auntie! Come to move in with you," Matt said, loud enough for the neighbors to hear.

CHAPTER 14

THE TEMP

Very late on Thursday afternoon, Pauline got a call at the Post Office to come into San Xavier early Friday morning for in processing. She was to start working at the Building Inspection division immediately after the paper work was completed. Pauline was still concerned about her cover, and brought it up to her boss. Pauline's boss, Mr. Mead, assured Pauline if her parents called the Post Office for any reason, he would pass the message along to Pauline immediately. Any calls from Pauline's coach, Sam, he would pass along as well. Pauline wanted her family and friends to think she was still employed at the Post Office, (technically she still was), so she wouldn't have to explain taking a lower paying job, after only one month at the Post Office.

Thursday evening, Pauline had a game. The current short stop, Marilyn Branson, called in sick, due to a family crisis, and Pauline got to play shortstop. Rumors started flying as quickly as those fly balls, that Pauline might have the job permanently, as the Coach was getting sick of Marilyn's lack of loyalty to the team. This was just fine with Pauline. Oh, how she wanted it. Bus she would have to wait to find out. The coach wasn't going to do anything about it today.

On Friday morning, May 17, 1985, Pauline's official start date, Pauline was considered an official San Xavier City employee. After spending the early morning processing incoming paperwork in the Personnel department, Pauline walked over to the Building Inspection department, one block away. Even though she was there to solve a mystery, she was looking forward to working in Building Inspection. Building Inspectors were employed by the city to test any new buildings built in San Xavier for building code violations.

As Pauline walked, her thoughts returned to the little in-processing room she was just in. It just didn't feel right. The tension had vibrated off the walls, and returned to her. You could cut the tension with a knife. One foot on the City's grounds and a cloud of apprehension enveloped her, and wouldn't let her go, until she stepped off the City owned property. "I wonder, if this means, that my sixth sense, is telling me that there is more going on in this City, then just as ex-building inspector taking kickbacks. However, it will be embarrassing for the big wigs at the City, when I crack this case, and it hits the papers. Do I really and truly want a career, with this place?" Pauline wondered to herself.

Pauline met the secretary of the Building Inspection Office. She'd be working under her, and Pauline's apprehension increased. Apparently, Pauline made the secretary nervous and apprehensive.

"Oh, hi! I'm Madeline Montgomery," the secretary introduced herself. "I told Personnel, I could handle this on my own, with Sheila on maternity leave, but Personnel didn't believe me. Don't get any ideas, about taking over my job!"

"Oh, no!" Pauline replied engagingly, "I'm only here to learn."

"Well, the first thing you do is to type this report, over there on that electric typewriter. I'm sure you don't know how to use our sophisticated word processing program. Temps never do," replied Madeline despairingly, emphasizing the word "sure."

Pauline not willing to argue, quietly took the handwritten

report written by the Chief Building Inspector over to the corner, to type it on the electric typewriter. It was the absolutely worst handwriting, she had ever seen, but Pauline quietly suffered through it without a word.

Finally, Madeline left for lunch, and Pauline was alone in the office. Pauline started going through the paper files to see if she could find anything that would incriminate Bill, the old Building Inspector, and or Joe, the contractor. She didn't find anything incriminating, but she did find out the same contractor that Matt mentioned earlier, Joe Bloom of XYZ, Inc., that built the Post Office buildings, also had an office in San Xavier, and had built office buildings in San Xavier. Joe had also worked on San Xavier's fairly newly built Post Office.

She also noticed that Bill Graham was listed as the City of San Xavier's building inspector for Joe's Bloom's buildings in San Xavier, on the old documents that she found in the files. Pauline rushed down the hall to the copier, and quickly made copies of them all. Pauline put the copies in her briefcase that she had bought for the occasion, and then quickly sat down at the typewriter. She wanted to appear, that she had been busy working on the report all along, when Madeline walked in from lunch.

"Still at it, I see," Madeline said arriving back from lunch. "You should be done with it by now, but temps, I mean temporaries are always so slow."

Pauline realized that Madeline knew no one could ever read the rough draft that Madeline gave Pauline to type from. This was okay with Pauline, since it would give Pauline an excuse to work slowly. Pauline wanted to appear dumb and slow, so she could work more hours into looking through the files.

"Oh, I guess that I'm just slow," Pauline said quietly. She added, "Oh, I'm meeting my boyfriend for lunch, at 1:00 p.m. He should be arriving soon."

"Oh, a boyfriend. How interesting. Tell me all about him."

Pauline thought that the old bat, probably just wanted to appear at least somewhat social. And she was old, at least 2 decades older than Pauline, and in Pauline's young mind, that's old.

Pauline knew that she had to make stuff up, based on the

cover that Mr. Mead told her about, "Well, he's the nephew of my old boss at San Xavier's Post Office, Mr. Mead's nephew, not his wife's. He's staying with the Meads for a while. He's a freelance writer, who is gathering research on Arizona's Mexican restaurants, so he can write an article for a travel magazine. I guess, Arizona is more exotic, than we natives, think. Matt, came all the way, from Washington, DC."

Just then Matt walked through the door, wearing a white cowboy hat that he bought at a Scottsdale 5th Avenue shop. The hat was adorned with a huge turquoise stone mounted on its white brim.

"Hi, Honey," Matt said. Pauline liked the sound of that. He continued, "I was walking down the street, and I saw a wild desert rose bush growing in the median of San Xavier's finest street. I picked a light pink rose bud for you."

"Why, gee, thanks. I'll just put it in this vase, that Sheila, left here, under her desk," Pauline wondered why couldn't he buy flowers, from a flower shop, like everyone else? At least it wouldn't be so cheap, and more romantic.

Matt asked, "Pauline, where should we go to lunch, Honey?"

"Why, Matt," Pauline said hastily taking his arm, and unobtrusively guiding him out the door, "You know we are eating Mexican, of course. Getting tired of it myself. Bye Madeline."

As they were walking down the street towards the Mexican restaurant three blocks away, Matt asked, "Why the Mexican restaurant routine?"

"That's your cover, I made up for you. Your Mr. Mead's nephew, from Washington DC, as you know. You're staying with him, while you are writing a freelance article on fine Arizona Mexican restaurants, for a travel magazine. You had to have some job. People your age don't stay weeks at a time, with their uncle, on vacation. They have to be working, and earning a living."

"Oh, great I now have to eat Mexican, as long as I'm here. Hopefully, we'll wrap it up soon, and it won't be for long. Fine Mexican restaurants, huh. I guess I won't be eating any fast food Mexican, either. No Taco Bell for me!"

"Oh, Matt, just remember your cover, and stop complaining," Pauline wondered, if she got a boyfriend, why did it have to be this one. She continued, "What's with the hat? Nobody **I know** owns a cowboy hat!"

"Oh, Pauline, isn't that the tourist thing to do for Easterners? Go Western once they get here. It will go well with my cover," Matt continued, "Speaking of cover I rented an expensive little red sports car. It will fit in better with my cover. Tomorrow we'll take her to lunch, instead of walking down the street to the fine Mexican restaurant."

"A little red sports car! That's great," said Pauline.

After ordering lunch at the restaurant, they got down to business. Matt told Pauline, about Ed, Evelyn, and Maggie. He told her about lunch with Maggie, but left out the wild goose chase with Ed. He did, however, mention Ed's nephew in Philly, Rick Klein-Hopper. He told her about the chemist, and the doctored soil and hydrological reports. He also told her about seeing Bill, and the contractor, Joe Bloom in Philly.

He also told her a little about Bill, from what he knew about him, from working with him for one day. He told her how strangely unmanly was Bill's frightened reaction to mice droppings that he had found on his Post Office's computer.

"Bill is a wimp. I haven't seen Bill, since he quit the Post Office. I expected to seem, him in Philadelphia for the building inspectors' convention, but I didn't. None of the San Xavier building inspectors came for that. Bill would have been working for San Xavier, at that time."

"It's a good thing, you never met any of the San Xavier's building inspectors, or it would have blown your cover, as a freelance writer."

"Yea, but you didn't know that I never met them! Before, you add anything in this story, you dreamed up, better check with me first! I'm the professional, remember. By the way did you find out anything this morning? Speaking of building inspectors, did you met any of them? And who is this Sheila person you mentioned earlier?"

"One question at a time. Sheila is the woman on maternity leave, whom I'm taking over for. Madeline Montgomery is the secretary for the building department. From what I gathered from reading her personnel file, which was in the office, she has been around forever. The old battle-ax! And no, I have yet to meet any of the building inspectors."

Pauline went on to tell him,that when Madeline was at lunch, she sifted through the files, and found out that Joe Bloom, was the main contractor in town, when Bill worked for the City. Bill had inspected all of the buildings built by XYZ, Inc., including San Xavier's Post Office. She gave Matt the copies of the documents that she had copied earlier.

"Yes, I remember, now. My boss decided not to have me check out San Xavier, after it was built. He said, he was going to trust the City's building inspectors in San Xavier. Gee, I'm going to get all this down. Let me pull out my notebook." In a whisper Matt continued, "I'll pretend I'm that restaurant critic, of yours, putting critique notes, in my notebook."

"Maybe, your boss, Herbert Reinhardt, is a suspect too, Matt."

"Herbert? Cost the government money! He has a fit, if I spend more than the government's statistical allowance on travel expenses. I stayed at a fancy hotel here, and I have to pay back the Post Office, the difference. Same thing with my sports car rental."

"Well, anyway, I still say, consider him a suspect. We will have to go to lunch, at 1:00 p.m. again. This way I can sift through the computer files, while Madeline is at lunch. She thinks that I'm so dumb, that I don't know how to operate one. Wait 'til she learns I aced my employment test on the computer. I don't like her, very much."

"She's just jealous, 'cause you're pretty and smart, and she's not."

"You think I'm pretty and smart, Matt?" Pauline asked.

"Yes, and don't let it to your head, Miss Detective."

"Oh, yes, Mr. Professional. We have to get back. If I'm late Madeline will have me for lunch!"

CHAPTER 15
THE COWORKERS

On Friday, Pauline met the current building inspectors, one man, and one woman. Pauline brought up the rumor she heard from Sam, her softball coach, about Bill, but she couldn't get anyone to bite, even Madeline. They all changed the subject on her, or claimed they couldn't remember the incident.

"Well," thought Pauline, "I can't get any information this way, maybe, if I hang around the employee lounge for a while, I'll pick something concrete up."

On her break, Pauline entered the employee lounge quietly. The lounge is an old house that had been converted. San Xavier city's offices had been growing so fast, because like all the Southwestern cities, there had been a population boom that the government had no time, to put up a building of its own. They had just bought an old house that someone had moved out of.

Pauline entered the house so quietly, that she startled two uniformed police officers that had been eating their lunch. Pauline was visiting the lounge, while Madeline was off somewhere for lunch. The police officers were discussing their day, and after they looked up at Pauline, they ignored her.

"Yea," said Officer Greg. "I lost my wallet down the City's sewer system. I noticed a manhole cover was knocked off, and I stopped to put it on. The wallet somehow fell out of my pocket, and into the drain."

The other officer laughed, and asked, "Did you check with Wastewater, maybe, they found it? Could have reached the lift station, by now. You are always driving off, and leaving your gas cap, on the roof of your patrol car, too, aren't you?"

"Yes, I checked with Wastewater. No luck. Besides it would be soggy, by now. And yes, I canceled my credit cards, and got a duplicate driver's license. And like, **you** never drove off, and left your gas cap, sitting on the pump. Don't laugh. This could easily happen to you, too."

"Not hardly!" replied Officer Greg.

Pauline pipes up, tired of being ignored. "I'm Pauline Schmidt. Nice to meet you. I'm working as a temporary for

Sheila in Building, while she's on maternity leave. I want to work my way into the Police Department, as a temporary clerk, typist, and then maybe, later, I can turn that into a Police Officer position." Pauline wondered if maybe, after all she really didn't want to join these inefficient officers, but it was already out of her mouth.

Officer Bob replies, "Well, none of our lady police officers, ever **lost** their wallets down the sewer drain. By all means, go for it!"

"Gee, thanks. I think," Pauline replies.

She decides to leave, as she realizes that this group of officers would not be able to shed any light on the building inspection mystery, as they can't even keep track of their own driver's license, that's floating down the Wastewater's underground river.

On the way, back to Building Inspection, Pauline passes the police property room building, where the stolen bicycles are kept. The room is unlocked and wide open, with no one around.

"Hello!" Pauline cries, looking into the room to see if anyone was there. There was no one around.

Pauline had no choice, but to call the Police Department, when she got back to Building Inspection. She didn't want to be labeled a troublemaker, but with the door wide open, anyone could steal a recovered bike, all over again. The sergeant at the desk thanked her for the information. He told her that it happened, all the time, but the employee in charge of the property room was related to the Police Chief, and it was hard to fire him. They were working on the problem.

"Is this like they fired Bill Graham for sexual harassment, when he was really taking kickbacks? Is that what working on the problem, means?" Pauline asked the Desk Sergeant over the phone.

"No," replied the Sergeant, "That's not what working on the problem means. Working on the problem means persuading the Chief that his 3rd cousin twice removed on his mother's side, is a Dodo Bird. And where did you hear the rumor about Bill? Surely not from a City employee?"

"No, my softball Coach, Sam, told me, about it. He heard it from his cousin, the building inspector."

"Which inspector, Joe or Amy?" asked the Sergeant?

"Joe Canary is the Coach's cousin. Well, how about it?"

"How about what?" the Sergeant asked playing dumb.

"Do you know anything about this kickback scandal? It's not a secret anymore, the whole softball league knows about it by now. Sam can't keep a secret."

"I don't know a thing. Before my time," said the Sergeant.

Pauline knew that, that was not true, as Madeline had told her that Sergeant Bob Randall, the Desk Sergeant, had been there forever, just like she had. In fact, Madeline wanted Pauline to know that she had the second highest seniority in the City, second only to Sergeant Bob. Pauline knew that paranoid Madeline told her this, so Pauline would know that there was no way she could steal Madeline's job, with all that seniority.

Pauline decided not to call the Sergeant on his blatant lie, and said good-bye. Besides Madeline would be coming back from lunch, soon, and Pauline had to get some work done, even if it was a minimal amount of work.

After work Pauline met Matt for dinner. Matt made it clear that they were meeting only to discuss the case. Pauline told her Mom not to expect her for dinner, that she was meeting friends from her church group. This time, Matt picked Pauline up from the City, and drove her in Matt's rented little red sports car to the same Mexican restaurant that they had just visited for lunch yesterday.

Matt was chattering along in the car, and Pauline started daydreaming. She noticed Matt's sea green eyes that seemed to reveal the depths of the ocean. Visions of her romance novel came back to haunt her..." Matt's words were like sugar coated dew drops, fresh and clear, like a green spring morning, words to be treasured in the secret recesses of her heart. His green eyes always sparkled like the sun bouncing off the foaming sea, whenever he spoke to her. Whenever she spied her true love, Pauline's heart within her lovely bosom would beat with wide anticipation." It was her discarded novel that starred a character named of all things, Matt.

Pauline realized her bosom certainly wasn't heaving with anticipation every time she saw the real Matt. Pauline was thrown out of her dreamlike state, by Matt asking her, if she thought his view of his penny pinching miserly boss, Herbert Reinhardt was correct.

Startled, Pauline thought, "Oh, my. I got to get a life. I'm day dreaming again. It was a good thing that I tossed that romance novel in the dumpster. What a flight of fantasy! We don't even live near a sea cliff anyway. "

Coming to the party at last, she answered Matt, "No, Matt. I think Herbert Reinhardt is a suspect. This miserly thing is all an act. He was always in on this thing."

"Well, you're wrong," bit back Matt, while turning the corner hard in his red sports car, "My boss is a cheapskate!"

"Yes, I know. Of course, I'm wrong. You're the professional," Pauline said sarcastically.

Pauline then smiled at Matt, trying hard to make up for her harsh words. Maybe, her girlfriend, Liza was right; she would only be curling up with the Post Office at night. She would be an old maid forever, and never marry unless she started doing things differently. And the first thing to do differently was learning how to flirt. Pauline would never curl up with anyone under the covers, without first being married to him in the Church, so learning how to flirt was essential, to catch a man. She wasn't going to demean herself by throwing herself into bed with Matt to catch a man, so she had to make Matt, fall in love with her, before he left her for Washington. "Got to replace that romance novel, with a book on how to flirt, from the San Xavier library," thought Pauline.

Pauline spent the whole dinner trying to flirt with Matt, the best she knew how, and wondered how to get a man to fall in love with her. She also slid some business in. She told him how she asked everyone around, about the kickback rumor, and they all claimed ignorance.

While at dinner, Pauline suddenly noticed Liza in the dark corner sitting on the red upholstered seats, with of all people, Tom, from the church group. "Well, that little snip," thought Pauline. "She knows I like Tom, and that means mitts off! I bet it was a call from Tom that she was waiting for that one Saturday, when I asked her to go to the mall, and she refused to go with me. But I noticed she didn't tell me that! Oh well, I have Matt, now. It doesn't matter." Pauline smiled an engaging smile at Matt, but deep down she was fuming over Liza and Tom.

Liza and Tom suddenly got up to leave, and came over to Pauline's table to say hello. Liza flipped her long curly brunette hair over her shoulder, as if to say, he's mine, so there, and said to Pauline, "Hi, Pauline. Tom and I were just having dinner, and we saw you here. Just came over to say, Hello." Liza, of Mexican descent, herself, a Hispanic, fit right in with the exotic ambiance of the restaurant.

Pauline responded in kind by flipping her long black hair which she usually wore straight but was curled today for Matt's sake, over her shoulder, and said, "Meet my new boyfriend, Matt Grayson. He's the nephew of my Post Office's boss, Mr. Mead. He's staying with the Mead's, while he writes a freelance travel article on Mexican dining in the Southwest. I'm helping him with research. Matt, this is my old friend Liza, and Tom, from church. Matt is a churchgoer, too, you know, there in Washington, DC, where he lives. He's going to move here soon, you know."

"You can drop the old part, Pauline. I'm not ancient," Liza said giggling softly and femininely, while extending her hand to Matt. Pauline glared as Matt, shook Liza's hand. Pauline was also glaring at fair-haired, blue-eyed Tom. Tom didn't say one word.

After Liza, took her leave with Tom, Matt said, "What's this he's going to move here soon, you know, bit? I thought I asked you to check with me, before you added to the story. That part wasn't necessary, to make the cover believable."

"I'm sorry," said Pauline crushed. Pauline was hoping he would move here. "It just kind of slipped out, you know."

"Well, just kind of not let it just slip out again, you know. Your grammar is atrocious. And didn't you tell your friends and family, you were working at San Xavier?"

"No, I didn't. I change out of Postal employee uniform at a gas station on the way to work every day to hide it from Mom. My Mom would wonder why I was leaving such a good job, for a temporary position. Working under cover, I couldn't tell her the truth. Couldn't tell my friends either. I would have had to admit, that I gave up my career plans with the Post Office, after only one month. It's bad enough that Mr. Mead is telling my coworkers at the Post Office, that I couldn't cut it. This assignment won't last that long anyway. If Liza and Tom knew the whole truth they would blab it all over town."

"Yes, Pauline," Matt said. "You are a good detective, to keep it all under cover. You did the right thing, a real pro."

"Thanks, Matt," Pauline chirped, beaming with pride.

CHAPTER 16
ALWAYS LEARNING

On Saturday, Pauline told her Mom, that she was going to San Xavier's library, to check out books on Criminal Justice.

"Why books on Criminal Justice?" Pauline's Mom asked.

"You know; they're in my field, got to keep up with the new technology, just 'cause I graduated doesn't mean, I can't stop learning," Pauline replied.

"You sell stamps at the Post Office. What do you mean your field? You'll never use your Criminal Justice degree," replied Mom.

"Just 'cause my first job, out of college is stamp selling, doesn't mean I'll never use it. Watch me," retorted Pauline.

At San Xavier's library, Pauline checked out books on man catching, instead of the books on Criminal Justice; however, she did read through the magazines on the criminal justice system. She also interrogated the poor cornered City librarians about what they knew about poor Bill, the ex-building inspector.

"Lady," said Mrs. Booker the librarian, "Librarians traditionally hang around books, not other city employees. I don't know anything. Leave me alone, and check out your books."

Pauline dutifully checked out her books went home and gobbled her way through each book, reading intently for the rest of the day.

On Sunday, Pauline saw Liza and Tom holding hands and sitting close to each other in the pew at church. The church building was underground as to save money on Arizona's air-conditioning costs. It was seventy-five degrees all year around inside the church. All that was needed to keep it at this temperature was a fan going for circulation, no air conditioner required. The church had grass growing on top of it. Water between the inner and outer wall, insulated the building. You could drive right by it, and not even see the church. All one could see was a grassy hill, with a cross reaching heavenwards. The church reminded her of the stories she had read about the ancient catacombs. "Catacombs, just like my life, hidden," thought Pauline.

Pauline had thought of asking Matt, to go with her to church, but he probably would not be able to find it, and since he wasn't Roman Catholic, probably wanted to go to a nondenominational church like the one he attended in Washington. "He probably went with the Meads to their nondenominational church," thought Pauline.

Pauline obviously and conscientiously ignored Liza and Tom, and she continued to spy on them in the underground church, all during Mass. Still fuming about Liza's capture of Tom, Pauline thought, "If I couldn't end up with Tom, why couldn't I end up with Detective Len. At least Detective Len is Catholic. "Why couldn't I end up with him? There are certainly enough Catholic men in this state."

Pauline knew that Arizona being a border state with Mexico had a large Catholic Mexican population, although Len wasn't Mexican. But there certainly were a lot of those dark, handsome Spaniards that she found appealing roaming around the city. She didn't have to end up with fair-haired, blue-eyed Tom.

Pauline spent the remainder of Sunday afternoon, at home, devouring her library books on man hunting. She paid careful attention to the book entitled, *How to Flirt Successfully*.

On Monday, Madeline mentioned to Pauline that she wanted her to clean up the archives.

"What are the archives?" Pauline asked.

"That's an old converted house, the city bought, that's located a mile from here. That's where all the records go, that we don't have room to store around here. We keep them there, because we don't need immediate access to them. We have to keep them somewhere, because the State Department of Library, Records, and Archives, requires us to keep all building records for at least one decade back, some records even longer."

"Oh," said Pauline. "I noticed some records were missing in your computer files, for some years. They must be paper files. That's where they are at."

"I thought that you didn't know how to operate a computer?" Madeline asked.

"I don't. I was just in the computer, in the tutorial section, trying to learn it," Pauline lied. She wanted to keep up the front that she was stupid.

Madeline excused herself, and went to the ladies' room.

Just then the janitor came in and started emptying the garbage. Pauline noticed that he was reading everything in it, before he threw it away.

"Why are you reading everything in the garbage?" asked Pauline.

"I always read everything in the garbage, before I throw it. Been doing it ten years now, ever since I first started. All the janitors do that. Nobody tells you nothing around here. Only way you learn anything is by going through the trash."

"Really, what do you learn?" Pauline asked the janitor.

"Oh, lots of interesting stuff. Could write a detective novel, about what I learn. I learned last year that they were planning on cutting positions. Mine was not one of them, but I had a lot more easier night sleeps, than my coworkers 'cause I knew before them, that mine was not in the frying pan."

"What kind of detective stuff, do you learn?" Pauline pumped him.

"Well, there was a building inspector named Bill a few years back. Found out they talked a young teenager on some kind of high school work-study program that they had working here, into saying that she was verbally harassed by Bill, so they could fire him. Real reason they wanted to fire him, was 'cause he was taking kickbacks from some contractor in Philadelphia. They could never prove it though. They should have gone through the garbage, though. I found some interestingly suspicious ledgers, though, that I kept. I'm taking Accounting classes; I know they were important."

"What did you do with these ledgers?" Pauline asked offhandedly.

"Well, I put them in a plastic bag. I was going to take them home, with me. Before I knew it; however, Sheila had bundled them up, and took them to the archives. Knowing how lazy Sheila is, I am sure they are still unsorted sitting in the archives, next to the pile of memos that she also took with her."

"Oh, isn't that interesting. Did you tell anyone about this?"

asked Pauline.

"Of course, not. Janitors are invisible. We're not supposed to know anything about what's going on around us. We're not supposed to repeat phone calls that we've overheard. Supposed to be unobtrusive. If they knew, I was reading their garbage, they would have me fired."

"How come you told me?" asked Pauline.

"Oh, temps are different. Here today, gone tomorrow, especially if Madeline has anything to say about it. She's paranoid. Been that way ever since the layoffs, I told you about. Temps are kin with janitors, around here, invisible."

"Invisible," said Pauline. "O.K., I'll keep that in mind. You better get back to work. Here comes Attila the Hun right now."

The nameless janitor got back to work, and Madeline came barreling in. "Ran into my boss in the hallway. He says I got to treat temps right from now on. He says that I can't give them jobs, that I would not do myself. He says you're dressed up too much, to go wading through some dusty archives, putting everything in order. Guess I got that job, now. This is all your fault! Every temp before you had to do this job! I hate you!"

"Oh, Madeline," says Pauline in a calming voice. "I would be happy to reorganize the archives. You can't do that in that beautiful suit you're wearing."

The janitor is laughing softly to himself, as he leaves the room.

"You're right. I'm not going to do it today. Maybe, I'll get to it, say four weeks from now, after I do the important stuff. Maybe, I'll let the returning mother do it. She has the key to the archives, in her desk drawer, somewhere. God only knows where that is. I'm so mad at you. Go on break or something, and leave me in peace for a while."

Pauline leaves quietly, and as unobtrusively as possible. She heads over to the employee lounge frustrated by her close attempts of solving this case. Even lowly city temps get a work break. Madeline leaves for her lunch soon after.

"I got to get into that archive, somehow," she thought. Entering the employee lounge, she discovers

Detective Len Browse, sitting quietly brooding over something.

He looks up. "Why, Pauline, what are you doing here? I though you worked for the Post Office?"

Pauline was tempted to share with Len, all things concerning her exciting case; however, she resisted. She remembered that Mr. Mead had told her the police must not know.

"I'm working as a temporary in the Building Inspection divisions, while Sheila is on maternity leave. I hope to move into being a temporary in the Police department, now that I'm on the temp. list. Ultimately, my goal is to get into police psychology or become a criminal analyst. I have a double major in Criminal Justice and Quantitative Methods from Arizona State University, and I want to use it."

"Why two degrees? Never heard of combining Criminal Justice and Quantitative Methods," asked Detective Len.

"I'm thinking of being a Crime Analyst. I thought, maybe, I could use it in manpower development. … Forecasting crime waves and needed personnel."

"Manpower development, that's what San Xavier needs, real

badly. You know, we are still too small to hire forensic technicians, and I have to do be an expert in police work, forensics, and psychology. For instance, you know the grisly murder you read in the paper yesterday?"

"Yes, it was gross. It was done, at someone's home in San Xavier."

"Yep, that's the one. My partner and I are assigned to the case."

"Well, it breaks my heart. After obtaining permission from the deceased victim's sister, I'm looking throughout the backyard looking for the murder weapon, the gun. Trying to dig up holes, and everything, and the sister of the victim is following me around like a puppy dog, on my tail every minute crying, and sobbing, and looking for comfort. I can't concentrate on the people end, and look for physical clues, at the same time. I'm good at looking for physical clues, but I'm not good at counseling, and interviewing. I don't want to ignore her, as I need to interview her later. Never taken any real psych classes."

"I've got a couple of suggestions."

"Shoot."

"Well, since the San Xavier manpower division, isn't good at training you to do both, divide the work. Your partner can talk to the victims, and distract them, while you look for weapons. Or you could talk to the sister, first, and get a search warrant to come back, when the house is empty. Or get a key from the sister, and ask her for permission, to come back later and look around, when no one's at home. Or you can sign up for classes on your own, or go talk to the Police chaplain. He knows about people. You can't be all things, to all people. San Xavier can't expect that."

"Boy, would you make a good detective! Got any more ideas?"

"Yes, you could suggest a program, like I saw on the news in California, where psychology interns from the university, ride along, and stay longer after the Police leave, in order to counsel the victims. They're all volunteers, so all it would cost the city is the salary for a volunteer coordinator."

"Wow, what a good idea! I would have thought of these ideas myself, but as you can see, I am emotionally upset right now, over this murder case. You've calmed me down, so I can think now. Thank you." A little tiny tear trickles down Len's cheeks.

Pauline upset that Len was so sad, but touched by his amount of genuine compassion, was very glad that she could make him feel better. She realized; however, that she must be getting back to Madeline, the old hag.

"I've got to go back to Building, now, but you hang

in there Len. I'll say a prayer. Maybe my suggestions will help you solve the case. Got to go. Bye."

"Bye Pauline," said Detective Len.

Pauline took a leisurely fifteen minute walk back to Building, stopping at the ladies' room, and the water fountain along the way, biding her time, dreading to see Madeline again.

The room is empty. As she walks in, the telephone rings.

"Building Inspection. This is Pauline. How can I help you?"

"This is Lt. Columbusa. Just want to say thanks."

"Thanks for what?"

"I hear that you've been helping my employees, feel better. Just heard it. Just wanted to say thanks, and please continue. I hope you stay working here a long time."

Pauline was so stunned that all she could say was, "You're welcome."

"Well, that's all I wanted to say. Good-bye," said Lt. Columbusa in his short stoppy cadence.

"Good-bye," says Pauline.

Pauline digs out the organizational chart in a hurry, and reads that Lt. Columbusa is in charge of the detectives. She thinks to herself, "Boy, that news travels fast, and I didn't make the most of my opportunity. Should have asked for a job as a detective, or at least a police clerk. Len, must really like me, if he said something to his boss. Wait a minute. If this news, gets around so fast, how come nobody seems to know what happened to poor Bill Graham, ex-building inspector? Something's fishy in this state of Denmark."

Pauline; however, was really touched by Len's actions. She didn't concentrate too long on solving her case of the missing Bill. She was more concerned that she had ended up lying to Len. After all, she never mentioned she was also still employed at the Post Office. Len would eventually see her there again selling stamps. What would she say? She began to wonder if she was such a good detective, after all, despite what Len had said, if she couldn't even cope with being "undercover."

She thinks to herself, I hate submerging my true identity. I wonder if Len hates this too, when he does it. Oh, maybe this will bring us close. We have something in common now."

While Pauline's muses these things over, Madeline walks in, and says, "Well, got no work done, as usual, I see. I am through with lunch. You can go at any time. Didn't you say you were meeting your boyfriend for lunch?"

"Huh?" says Pauline, she was still thinking that at least at this job, she didn't have to wear an ugly blue uniform, like everyone else.

"You who, Pauline, you dreamer, wake up! Do you want to go to lunch now, or not?"

Pauline looking at her watch, "Oh, yes, it's almost 1:00 pm.

Got to meet Matt, at the Mexican restaurant at 1:00."

"Isn't that what I just said?" Madeline asked.

"Well, got to go. Good-bye Madeline. See you after lunch."

"Dippy girl," says Madeline gently to herself, after Pauline is out of earshot.

Pauline walked down to the Mexican restaurant by herself. Matt and she had decided to meet, rather than having him pick her up. "After all," Pauline had chided him the last time they were together. "In real life, other people's boyfriends aren't quite that attentive. We don't want to arouse suspicion."

When Pauline laid eyes on Matt at the restaurant, she forgot all about Len. Matt was already seated, when Pauline came running up to meet him with open arms. Concentrating on her man hunting advice gleaned from library books, she cried, "Oh, Matt, Matt, Matt, darling!!! Can't wait to tell you my news!" while landing a fire engine red lipsticked kiss on his cheek, and engulfing him with a huge hug.

"Carrying this 'boyfriend-girlfriend' thing, a little too far, aren't you? Whispered Matt. "I thought you said too much attentiveness was suspicious?"

"Oh, I guess I did say that on Friday, didn't I?" Pauline whispered remembering her pre-library conversation with Matt. "I'll behave myself. I'm sorry. It's just that you're so lovable."

Pauline wished she had never said attentiveness was too much, especially, now after her favorite author said it was necessary for every great relationship.

"What's the news?" asked Matt, ignoring the lovable comment.

Pauline proceeds to sit down at the table, and tells him all about her conversation with the janitor including the ledgers, and the archives.

"Good work, Pauline! Everyone forgets the janitors, and they are the most important people to interview. Those ledgers are the key. We need them in order to put out warrants for Bill, and the contractor," Matt says excitedly.

Pauline beams. She continues, "But how am I going to get them? You are being premature about the warrants. Maudlin Madeline subsequently took me off archive duty."

"Take the key! Call in sick, and go look for them. You are an employee. You won't be stealing the key, and you're allowed on City property. I'm not," Matt pauses, "When you get back to the office, wait until Madeline leaves to use the ladies' room, and then call Sheila. She'll know where she put the key. You said you found her number in Madeline's personal files. You said Madeline has been in the ladies' room a lot lately, so that won't be a problem."

"What if Sheila is in labor, when I call? She's off, because she is getting ready to deliver. You're right about Madeline. No problem. She must have a bladder infection, or something. She's always in there."

"Just call Sheila, why don't you! And could we **please** talk about other subjects at lunch, besides the workings of females' anatomies!"

"Oh, Matt!" Pauline decided to dump those unhelpful library books, since everything she said backfired.

When Pauline returned from lunch, Pauline called Sheila and

found out that the key to the archives was at the bottom of the vase that Matt's now dead flower adorned. "God only knows, why she put it in there," Pauline thought. Sheila had not delivered, yet. When Pauline called, she found Sheila in the middle of baking brownies for Sheila's four year old. Sheila was very sweet to Pauline, and not upset at all for being interrupted at home.

Later that afternoon, Detective Len called to thank Pauline for helping him, on his new case. It seems Len lassoed a warrant, and went back, when the house was empty. He subsequently found the murder weapon, a pistol, by quietly digging under the small, immature peach tree in the backyard. He promised to keep Pauline up to date on future developments, as long as she was a fellow employee, and could be trusted to keep silent. "He owed it all to her," he said. Neither one mentioned the thank you call from Detective Len's boss, Lt. Columbusa.

Pauline had had enough of the library books. She had previously planned on checking them out again to reread, but since she already had the library books in her car she decided just to return them. On the way home from work, she dumped them off at the library.

CHAPTER 17
ANCIENT HISTORY

Pauline called in sick to Madeline on Tuesday. She had taken the key to the archive home with her, before she had left on Monday. She had also gotten directions to the archive from the janitor, before she had left on Monday.

Tuesday morning, Pauline quietly unlocked and opened the squeaky door to the renovated old house, which was used to store the City's old papers. The place obviously had not received too many visitors. Pauline coughed, and coughed, and coughed from the dust that she stirred up. The room was pitch black with only a little light streaming in from under the curtains. She tried to turn on the light at the switch, but nothing happened. She reached up towards the ceiling and pulled the pull to the overhead light, but still nothing happened. It was then that she realized that the City had turned off the electric, to save money. She went out into her car, to get her flashlight. Using the flashlight, she found her way into the house. She debated opening the curtains, but she didn't want to arouse suspicion from the police officers, that cruised by regularly, so she decided not to open them. "After all," she thought, "I'm supposed to be sick today."

After trying to wash her dusty hands from a kitchen sink, which she soon discovered had no running water, she roamed from room to room, looking for the plastic bag, that the janitor had described, so well. She couldn't find it. But in the very back room, there were shelves and shelves of building inspection files, and computer diskettes. She spent hours, and hours going through the files, finding nothing incriminating.

It was getting close to 1:00 p.m., the time she was supposed to meet Matt at the restaurant. "Matt will get worried pretty soon, but I must press on, and find something," Pauline told herself.

Finally, she spied the big, green, plastic bag like the ones the janitors used, tucked away in the corner of the shelf. She tugged, and tugged, and tugged, and finally drew it out, and sat cross-legged on the floor, with the flashlight poised above the bag. She opened the bag and oh la, la, the ledgers appeared. Uncomfortable without a chair, but overcome with the excitement of the moment she proceeded to read the ledger. It had the name Bill Graham on the ledger, and entries recorded from the Philadelphia contractor, Joe Bloom, of XYZ, Inc. "Looks like kickbacks to me!" thought Pauline. "Yea, huh, I cracked my first case!" she jumped up and waved the ledger excitedly around her head, dancing and screaming for joy.

Just then, she heard a loud thud in the front room, which used to be the living room of the old house. Pauline went running in to see what happened. Startled, she spies a portly, balding, pointy nose man lying on the floor, next to a sprung mouse trap, with a dead mouse in it. Pauline cried, "Oh, no! Help!"

No one is around to hear her. She assumes it's another San Xavier employee who came to clean up the archives, and got into trouble. She leans down to take his pulse. There is none. "Oh, no. Help! He's dead!" she cries again.

Just then Matt runs into the room ducking so not to hit his head on the threshold. "I heard your scream! What happened! You were so late; I came to check on you." He looks down, and spies the dead man. The light from the now opened door illuminated the pointy nose dead man. The small building's ceiling was so low that the pull from the light kept hitting Matt on the head. "Why that's Bill Graham. What happened to him?" Matt said in utter disbelief.

"He's dead! I checked his pulse!" Pauline screamed, grabbing Matt for support.

"Are you sure? Let me check," says Matt. Matt leans down to check the pulse.

"Are you sure? Let me check," Pauline chides, "What do you think I'm so stupid, I can't take a pulse. Took CPR, I did."

Matt stands up, after bending down to check the pulse.

"Now do you believe me?" Pauline asks. "O.K., pro, what do we do now?"

"We call the detectives, and tell them the whole story, whether the Post Office likes it or not."

"The whole story? I found the ledgers, you know, incriminating this dead man, and the contractor Joe Bloom.

What whole story? We don't even know who killed him, and now I won't even get the pleasure of seeing him arrested."

"Why, Pauline, you're so cold. A man is dead, who I used to work with. Granted it was only one day, but I used to work with him nonetheless. A fellow building inspector."

"Forget the violins. I will go hunt down some detectives. You stay here. There's no electric in this place, and consequently no phone."

Pauline gets ready to leave, as she walks toward her car, a marked Police car pulls up.

"We were driving by, and we noticed all this activity," says the Police Officer getting out of his car, "Usually the archive doesn't get cleaned, but once a year. What's going on?"

Pauline reading the hunky male officers' name tags stammered, "Oh, Officer Smitty and Officer Royal, it's kind of complicated. Go inside and talk to Matt. I'm going to wait outside here, and get some fresh air." Pauline starts coughing. She thinks to herself, "Let's see, ol' Matt explain this one. He's always rubbing it in."

Apparently, Matt did a good explanation job, because fifteen minutes later the officers resurfaced and talked to Pauline.

"We got the whole Post Office story from your partner. We hear you're working undercover at the City. Don't move. We want to hear your side. First, we are going to call the FBI, and the Post Office, and our own Personnel office to verify the story. We'll call in our own Detective Len Browse, and the County Coroner. We are still too small to have our own coroner," said Officer Smitty.

The police disappear for thirty minutes inside the patrol car in order to call out on the CB radio. Matt waited inside, and Pauline waited outside like she was told to do. When they returned from their car, they asked Pauline her side of the story. Basically, Pauline told him everything. It must have agreed with Matt's version, because afterwards, Officer Royal said, "Well, it agrees with your cohort's in the house. But stick around. You know, just because we believe your crazy story, doesn't mean both of you aren't considered murder suspects."

"What!" Pauline cried, "That's ridiculous."

"Just wait here, until Detective Len comes. The coroner will be here in fifteen minutes," Officer Smitty replies.

Matt stayed inside. Apparently the officers wanted to keep them separated. "Matt must be having fun, in there with only dead Bill to keep him company. Gross," Pauline thinks to herself.

Detective Len was surprised to see Pauline, to say the least. Pauline related the whole story to him. His response was, "You lied to me. You didn't tell me, a thing."

"I was undercover. The Post Office did not want the Police to know. You know what it is like to be undercover," Pauline pleaded for under-standing. "Great!" thought Pauline discouraged, "I'm losing another romantic prospect. First, Tom from church, now Len."

"Oh, I'm sorry. Yes, I do know full well, what it's like to be undercover. It ruins your social life. Forget dating," Len says.

"Oh, good," thought Pauline, "Something in common, after all."

Pauline beams back at Len, "Look at this!" she says, "We have something in common!"

Detective Len gets Pauline home telephone number, for the case he says. Pauline readily gives it to him, although she wonders how to explain all this to Mom, when Len calls.

Just then the coroner arrives. Matt finally comes out of the house. Pauline introduces Matt to Detective Len. Len interviews Matt and hears the whole story all over again.

"Well, you two must leave now. Don't leave town. I have to look at the physical evidence, now, for this murder. We'll turn over the ledgers to the FBI, so they can arrest Joe Bloom for taking kickbacks," Len says.

Pauline replies, "You don't think we are suspects, do you?"

"Uh, uh, well, of course not. But I'm a good detective, I have to leave all possibilities open."

"Oh?" said Pauline, "Well, you got my home number, Len."

She smiles a disarming smile at Len, and watches for any jealous reaction from Matt. There is none. They say good-bye to the detective, and to each other.

Matt gets into his shiny rented sports car, and drives off towards the Meads.

Pauline gets into her dull privately owned gray hardtop, and drives home.

CHAPTER 18
TAMING THE MIGHTY

Pauline came in a little early on Wednesday, to tell Madeline, the whole story. Madeline it seemed had already heard. Gail Bernside, from Personnel had called Madeline last night at home, to tell her the long tale. News traveled fast in that City.

"She said that you and your so called boyfriend Matt might be suspects in Bill's murder," Madeline said, quietly.

Pauline thought, "No wonder Madeline greeted me so nicely this morning. She's scared of me."

"Boo!" yelled Pauline at Madeline.

Madeline jumped back with a start.

"Gottcha. You don't have to be scared of me. I'm no murderer, just a lowly clerk. Matt's not either. Detective Len doesn't think so, either. You can just relax around me. Stop walking on egg shells."

"Me? No, I don't think you're a murderer," Madeline lied. "I'll be right back. I'm going to the ladies' room."

Pauline was alone and laughing to herself, when the custodian walked in to empty the trash. This was a different custodian, than the one Pauline had talked to earlier, a woman janitor this time.

"What's so funny?" asked Marigold, the custodian.

"Oh, nothing. It's just things are rarely like they seem."

"Tell me about it. Did you ever hear the story when the monsoon storm messed up the Public Works CB radio system, and the phone lines? Things really were not what they seemed on that day."

"No, I didn't hear the story. Tell me about it."

"Well, the wires got crossed. The Public Works

Secretary tried to call, my fellow custodian in vehicle #1111, from the base, and a telephone operator came on the line and said, 'twenty-five cents, please'. The secretary responded, shocked, 'Just where am I supposed to put it?' 'In the hole, of course,' said the operator. The secretary laughed and said, 'Operator. This is a city CB line. There is no hole. Get off my line. I have to use it.' The operator said, 'I don't believe you. And I warn you, if you continue to be nasty, I'm going to hang up on you.' And she did. It was so funny! All day the telephone would ring, and you would pick it up, and hear two Public Works workers talking over the CB. Vehicle CB's were picking up private telephone conversations between City employees. We found out what people were really thinking about their bosses. It was broadcasted!"

"How did the problem get solved? Did it affect any emergency calls!"

"No, by the grace of God. It was a slow day. The Emergency Police and Fire System were tied into different phone lines, under a separate system, so it didn't affect them."

Pauline laughingly said, "How did the problem get solved?"

"Well, the Public Works secretary called up the CB radio maintenance company, and they told her it was the phone company's fault, and they weren't coming to fix it. She called the phone company's maintenance division, and unlike the operator, they believed her, but blamed the CB radio company. The secretary then called them both back and threatened them with law suits for violating maintenance contracts, if they both weren't on the spot in less than an hour. And they better work together cheerfully, whether they wanted to or not! Since they were under the threat of lawsuit, they were nice as pie to each other, which was a first. They worked together to get the lines uncrossed. They used a map that the phone company had of the underground phone lines. The rain and mud from last July's flash floods had moved the lines a full two inches! Took them all day to fix it."

"My! That's so funny!" Pauline remarked. "The story of my life. My wires are always getting crossed!"

While the custodian, Marigold, and Pauline were having a hearty laugh, Madeline came back in. The custodian quietly left, and Pauline was alone with Madeline. Madeline was almost crouched in the corner. She pointed to a stack of files across the room, and said, "There Pauline. File those in the next room."

"O.K.," said Pauline. "And Madeline really, you don't have to be afraid of me." Secretly, however, she was glad to have tamed mighty Madeline.

After filing, Pauline left to meet Matt, for lunch. Since the rouse was off, Matt chose something else rather than

Mexican. They met at a booth at a local fast food hamburger joint.

"Why didn't the Police know what was going on in the building next to their own? They should have known about the kickbacks, and confiscated the ledgers," asked Matt.

"Because they were too busy looking for wallets in sewers, locking property room doors, and retrieving lost gas caps," Pauline answered.

"Say what?" said Matt.

"Never mind," said Pauline. "Just rethinking my career decision out loud. Let's just say the San Xavier Police Department is inefficient to say the least."

"Let's make up a murder suspect list, to give to Detective Len, since he definitely needs an old pro's guidance. Oh, and your help too, Pauline. I'll dig out my notebook. First thing that I learned, every case needs at least thirteen suspects, so I'll number my page, one to thirteen."

"But Matt, isn't that superstitious? That has no basis in fact. Thirteen is an unlucky number, anyway. What if the case doesn't warrant thirteen suspects?"

"Every case does warrant thirteen suspects. That's my point. It's my trade secret."

"Whatever. I give up. Number one suspect should be Joe Bloom of XYZ, Inc. He would want Bill silenced forever, the most. Put him down as number one."

"Okay, down he goes. Number two should be the chemist from Soil Analysis, Inc. He probable was paid to doctor the reports. Number two, current Peace Corp volunteer, Chris Sinkfeld."

"Okay, I agree, who is next?"

"Number three is Ed Brook, from Small Creek Post Office. He could have changed the reports, also, and wanted Bill silenced. Number four is Evelyn Brook for the same reason."

"Okay, I agree. Number five is Maggie Brook. She could have changed the reports, also. She had access to it."

"Oh, no, not sweet quiet Maggie. I refuse to put her down!"

"You put her down, Matt, or I am walking right now! Just because you said once that you dated her, does not mean she is exempt! Your judgment is clouded!"

"Stop screaming, Pauline! Okay, okay, I'll put her down as number five."

Pauline asked, "Number six?"

"Number six is Rick Klein-Hopper. He had a Post Office box in the same city as the contractor, and he ran a business from it. Ed was visiting him in Philadelphia, when I ran into him. Rick is Ed and Evelyn's nephew. Although my boss checked him out, called, and said Rick was clean, which leads me to start to wonder about my own boss, Herbert Reinhardt. Herb never told me what business Rick ran, and Herbert was working at the Post Office as Bill's boss, when Bill Graham was there, and it took him all this time to discover something was wrong? Also, by the looks of it the Small Creek Post Office has been sinking for quite some time now. All of this cannot be just government inefficiency?"

"Well, this is stupid, Matt. That's all you have to go on for your own boss. I know, I always suspected him, but now I don't know. Kind of circumstantial." Pauline kidded, "May as well include my own boss in that case, Mr. Mead. He knew about the high utility bills for a long time, now."

"Good idea, Pauline. Mr. Mead fills the number eight slot, Herbert Reinhardt, number seven."

"I was only kidding. You take him out! Do you want me fired!"

"Nope. He stays. Mr. Brown is number nine. He's the postmaster, slash grocery store owner, where Joe Bloom has his suspicious Post Office box."

"You'll go for anything won't you to fill your slots. There's no substance to it."

"Moving right along," Matt ignored her. "The president of Soil Analysis Inc., Robert Mitchus is next. He could have changed the reports too, and wanted Bill silenced. He could be in on the kickback scheme. Your turn. Got any ideas for eleven, twelve, and thirteen?"

"Nice you let me in on this Matt," Pauline chided, "Well, maybe it was one of the City employees. After all your chemist is out of the country with the Peace Corps. Your other suspects were in different cities, not even in the State of Arizona, at the time of the murder. Number eleven, could be Joe Canary, Building Inspector, after all he knew all about the sexual harassment charade. He told my coach about it, and he was employed at San Xavier, when Bill was there. For that matter, so were Sheila and Madeline." Pauline paused.

Matt said, "Do go on."

"Well, Madeline although I'd love to hang her, is too dumb to murder anybody. Sheila, however, for some strange reason hid the archive key, in the bottom of the flower vase, where no one could find it, even Madeline. Maybe, she did not want it found, because she knew the incriminating ledgers were in there. Sheila is number twelve. And the entire Police Department, except for Detective Len, of course, is number thirteen. They might have found out through Personnel that we were investigating, and didn't want to be embarrassed because they were so inefficient. They didn't want to be shown up, so they murdered Bill in cold blood."

"Well, the entire San Xavier Police Department, huh? Well, why not. They have us down as suspects. Okay, I'll put down number eleven, Joe Canary, Building Inspector, number twelve Sheila, and number thirteen the entire police department, **no one excluded**."

"I'll ignore that last remark," says Pauline. "Madeline gave me the afternoon, off. She's afraid of me. What should we do?"

"Let's drive over to the Post Office. We can call the FBI man, and see what he has found out lately. We'll set up a three way conference call, in Mr. Mead's office."

At the Post Office, Matt got permission from Mr. Mead to use his office. Matt asked Mr. Mead to leave, without explaining to him, that he was a suspect. Matt asked Pauline to cover her inquisitive ears, while he made the password call through the FBI switchboard.

"Hi, George. This is Matt Grayson, and Pauline Schmidt, who I told you about. She is listening in on the speaker phone."

"What! She heard the password! Now we have to change it."

"Relax," Pauline said, "Matt made me cover my ears. I didn't hear a thing."

"If you don't mind, we'll change the password anyways, just for precautionary sake."

"George, how do you think Bill heard about Pauline, in the archives? He must have come out of the woodwork to check up on her. He would not have been looking for those records, if he didn't know we were."

"Matt, he must have panicked. Not sure he threw them out. He would have known that all the old records back that far would have only been in the archives."

"But how did he hear about us investigating him?" Pauline asked.

"Matt, told him," George replied, "Indirectly."

"What!" exclaimed Matt.

"Yes, Matt, you and your big mouth. I did some investigating, of the suspects on my own. I talked to Ed and heard about your goose chase in Philadelphia. I investigated Rick Klein-Hopper, by the way. He was clean."

"What goose chase?"exclaimed Pauline, who had heard none

154

of this from Matt.

"Never mind, Pauline," Matt said, "Go on George."

"Well, Ed told Maggie, how he ran into you, and about your plans to check out San Xavier. I talked to Maggie, sweet girl, but very gossipy. She said she told her new boyfriend, a CPA with a major national accounting firm, the whole story. This boyfriend's, Fred Ames, main office is in Philadelphia. I interviewed Fred on the phone. It seems he told the whole story of how you jilted Maggie, to another accountant in the same firm, who worked in the Philadelphia office. He thought you were a real clown, and Maggie a great catch, so this story got told around the whole company. Anyway, this other accountant, I found out through my investigation, is the accountant assigned to XYZ, Inc., in fact, the accounting firm's number one client. This accountant, John Smith, told Joe Bloom, the whole story, not realizing of course, that Joe was the contractor in the story. Apparently, in this game of telephone tag, Joe's Bloom name was left out of the story by this point. Anyway, Joe Bloom must have alerted Bill, and Bill must have been there to double check, and make sure that all traces were accounted for. He was looking for the ledgers, not necessarily following you, Pauline."

"Whoa, that's a relief. I thought maybe he was planning on murdering me," Pauline said.

Matt said, "Maggie! Just like a woman to blab!"

"Excuse me! Who talked first!!" Pauline exclaimed.

"Matt, you do seem to not act like a pro. I would hardly blame the women. Especially after Pauline did such a fine job in investigating and uncovering the ledgers."

"Thank you, George," Pauline would always remember this comment by an FBI man.

"Anyway," said Matt. "This is not important. Bill is caught, alas dead. We should arrest Joe Bloom. He is the murderer."

"Too late, Matt. I already arrested him. In fact, I was arresting him, the same moment you found Bill dead. Soon after I had him booked for fraud, I received a call from your San Xavier Police Officers. The same ones who had parked outside the archives earlier."

Pauline and Matt together exclaimed, "You mean we missed it!" "It" meaning the arrest. Both wanted to be there.

"Yes, you two missed it. Amateurs not allowed. Anyway Joe is not the murderer. He was very busy at the time of the murder. And besides he wanted Bill to find the misplaced ledgers first."

"He could have hired it done," Matt said.

"How did you get enough evidence to arrest him without my ledgers I found? Don't you need them at all?" asked Pauline.

"Of course, we need them, Pauline, for a conviction. Like I said, good work. We got a warrant for the Greenwood Post Office box, and talked to the Postmaster there. He said Joe was a regular visitor who put ledgers in the giant sized box, the largest one he could rent, and never took anything out of it. We found ledgers detailing the kickbacks given for all of the Post Office buildings, and for the buildings in the City of San Xavier. I'm sure they will match up to the figures found in Bill's complimentary set," George said.

"Wow, good detective work!" said Matt and Pauline together admiringly.

"Thanks," replied George.

"I'm going to get some physical evidence to tie Joe Bloom's henchman to the crime. Please call the county coroner tomorrow, and pave the way for me to talk to him. Tell him I'll meet him at 1:00 p.m., in his office, tomorrow," Matt said.

"I want to come too," said Pauline. "Since Madeline thinks I'm the murderer, I'll just have to scare her a little, and she'll let me off to go too. I know it."

Matt replied, "Oh, that stupid Police Department has got Pauline and me as suspects. The whole City thinks we're partners in crime."

"That's ridiculous," replied George. "I didn't get that impression, when I talked to them last. I call Detective Len, back, and right now, and clear it up."

"Detective Len doesn't think so. He likes us. We are not suspects," Pauline said.

"She's just sweet on him. He does too, think we're suspects. You call him!" Matt pleaded with George.

"Matt, I am not sweet on him. He is just a nice guy and a good detective doing his job. I like you, not Detective Len." Pauline smiled a big flirtatious smile at Matt.

"Why, Matt?" George said.

"Just drop it, both of you!" Matt replied.

Pauline frowned, and pouted a sexy pout.

Matt glared at her, silent.

"Well, I call the coroner and the detective, and leave you two love birds alone. Call me later, after talking with the coroner and Detective Len."

"Good-bye, Edgar," said Matt.

"Edgar?" said Pauline. "Who's Edgar?"

"Good-bye Matt and Pauline," replied George. George hung up.

"Edgar," said Pauline to Matt. "Who's Edgar?"

"J. Edgar Hoover, of course," Matt replied referring to his running joke of referring to George as J. Edgar Hoover, ex infamous head of the FBI.

CHAPTER 19
FIRED!

Pauline came in early on Thursday morning to speak to Madeline, about leaving early to talk to the coroner. It seems that Madeline came in early as well, hoping to catch Pauline before the workday started. Madeline said to Pauline, as Pauline walked through the door, "You can leave at noon, today, Pauline. Your temporary status with us is over. I told Personnel that I didn't want a murder suspect working with me, and they agreed to send in someone new until Sheila returns. Sheila had a boy yesterday, by the way. Healthy too. Besides, you have completed the job, you were sent here for. You solved the kickback crime with the Post Office."

Pauline thought to herself, "Wicked old bat!" Instead she replied, "That's fine with me. I didn't murder anybody! But what about you! You were here when Bill worked here. Didn't you know about the kickbacks? Everyone knew how they got him fired for something else, when they all suspected the kickback scheme, but couldn't prove it."

"How dare you even think I knew anything, or had anything to do with Bill's murder! You're just averting suspicion! Here are some files. Now go file in the next room, away from me."

Pauline left quietly, but fuming. She filed until noon, and then she left quietly without saying good-bye to anyone.

Pauline still hadn't said anything to her parents. She did not want them to worry. Detective Len hadn't contacted her at home, so she didn't have to explain anything, yet. She thanked God that her parents didn't know.

Pauline met Matt as he was turning the corner of the hallway to get her. She told him about how Madeline was treating her like a criminal. Matt threatened to tell Madeline a thing or two, but Pauline told him that she was glad that he hadn't ran into her. Pauline just asked Matt to just go, and they left in a hurry.

They drove to downtown Phoenix, to visit with the county coroner. After the visit, Pauline and Matt discussed the coroner's conversation, on the way back to San Xavier, while riding in Matt's rented little red sports car.

"I guess Madeline didn't have to find a replacement for me, as such. I'm not the murderer. In fact according to the county coroner, there was no murder."

"Can you believe what he said, Pauline?"

"I can't believe he said that Bill died from a heart attack. Could it have been that dead mouse, we found in the mouse trap that brought it on? Didn't you tell me that Bill was deathly afraid of mice? The coroner said he had arteriosclerosis… A heart attack, frightened by a mouse," Pauline shakes her head, unbelievingly.

"I don't believe it," Matt replies. "I think it was poison, made to look like a heart attack."

"Well, he did say the aorta was completely blocked with fat deposits, and Bill did weigh in at about three hundred tons."

"That's true. And the coroner did track down Bill's doctor from the medical card he carried in his wallet, and confirmed, that Bill refused to follow the low cholesterol diet. Also, he refused to take his new cholesterol lowering medicine, because the medicine had just come out, and he was concerned over any, as yet undiscovered, possible side effects. And when I saw Bill eat last with Joe Bloom, he was shoveling it in."

"Matt, this means there is no murder left for me to solve!"

"But it does mean that we are off the suspect list, with Detective Len, and the San Xavier Police department. This is good news."

"Granted I would give anything to have Madeline eat her murderous words, but I still say it was poison or something. Matt you were a detective once. Let's make up a list of poisons to have Detective Len check on, and then give him the suspect list."

"Fine, I'll do it. You're right. Could have been poisons. I know a lot of poisons to list. Besides I want to see Detective Len's face, when we see he sees why we put him on our suspect list."

After parking in the San Xavier City's parking lot, Matt finished his poison list, and drew out the suspect list from his pocket. They walked into the Police Headquarters front lobby, and asked the desk Sergeant, Sergeant Bob Randall, the one Pauline tattled to about the property technician, if they could have Detective Len paged. Sergeant Bob complied giving Pauline a funny look and said, "You were the one I talked to on the phone, weren't you? Heard the whole story Pauline."

Detective Len was in his office when he heard the page, and came out into the front lobby to talk to them. "Why are you here?" Detective Len asked, "Didn't you hear that the coroner ruled it natural causes? And the FBI arrested Joe Bloom for fraud."

"Yes, we just came from the coroner's office. We think that it was poison that was used to make it look like a heart attack. We came up with a list of poisons and suspects. Here's the list." Matt handed the detective both lists.

Detective Len scanned both lists quickly and started laughing, "What's this? The entire San Xavier Police department. Let's see, and the motive, you have down here is embarrassment for not catching up with Bill sooner, and being one-upped by the Postal Service. Give me a break!" Len started laughing heartily.

"Hey, turnabout is fair play. You had both Pauline and me

down as suspects, and that was even more ridiculous!"

"Hey, you two!" Pauline interjected, "I am taking these lists seriously. I still say it was murder. Of course, I had nothing to do with putting down the San Xavier Police Department. I want you to know that Len." She smiled at him, and continued, "It was all Matt's idea you know. And I didn't put my postal boss's name on it either, so don't tell him that I did. I did leave out a name though, Madeline Montgomery. She kept calling me a murderer, after she heard that I was on your suspect list. Today was my last day with San Xavier. Madeline saw to that. Now I'll never know how your other murder case comes out Len, until I read about it in the newspaper."

Just then a dark haired stranger that was sitting in the dark corner of the police lobby hiding behind a newspaper comes rushing up to talk to the threesome. He introduces himself, as a newspaper reporter.

"I thought I shooed you away, earlier. I told you it was a slow news day," Detective Len says.

"Pauline, no, don't!" shouts Detective Len.

165

Before he could stop her, Pauline anxious to get her name in the paper as the heroine, tells the local newspaper reporter the whole story. The reporter takes a picture of Matt and Pauline, the heroes. Detective Len refuses to be in the picture. He still has undercover work left to do on other cases, and Matt was right, he was embarrassed about being one-upped.

The newspaperman promises Pauline, that it will all be in tomorrow's early morning edition of the *San Xavier Chronicle*, page one. Pauline is very excited.

CHAPTER 20
SUCCESS AT LAST!

Friday morning before going to work at the Post Office, Pauline got up early to buy a copy of the *San Xavier Chronicle*. The story was indeed on page one, just like the reporter said it would be, with the picture of her and Matt on it. They were listed as heroes in the discovery of the kickback scheme.

She decided to let the story do her talking for her, and showed the story to her parents. At first they were upset, as they worried about the peril, she put herself in. Next they were upset, that the Post Office wouldn't take her back, and she would be working as a low paying temporary with San Xavier forever. Pauline assured them that was not the case. After that, they saw it as a plus, something that would help her career. A career they hoped, as something safe behind a disk, like Police Planning, or maybe, Postal Inspecting.

"You know," Pauline said to them, "It amazes me how great the sum total of human knowledge is, and yet people can still be so stupid. Did Bill and Joe Bloom really think they would never be found out?" Then she added, "Then of course, if people weren't so stupid, the sum of human knowledge wouldn't be so great. There would be no crime, and hence no criminal psychology. With no crime, there would go all my future career plans. I can't wait until I show my friends the article in the *San Xavier Chronicle*."

Pauline's mother tired of her daughter's constant speeches, replied by hurrying her now late daughter off to work at the Post Office.

"I can't wait until I see Matt today, Mom. You'll like him, he's wonderful!" Pauline said leaving quickly so she wouldn't be so late.

All of her friends, at the Post Office treated Pauline like a hero. They had also read the paper that morning. Pauline's boss, Mr. Mead, congratulated her heartily, and promised he would do all he could to advance her career with the Post Office.

At lunchtime Matt stopped by the Post Office to say goodbye. Matt was looking forward to his quiet single lifestyle in his modern looking office, surrounded by the streetlights that looked like popcorn balls. Matt knew he had many long working nights ahead of him, with the light shining in from those moon glow street lamps.

Pauline, however, was convinced that Matt, would find a detective job with San Xavier, and move here to be with her forever.

Matt, however, dashes Pauline's unsaid hopes, by cavalierly mentioning that he is on his way home to Washington, DC with bachelor TV pizza dinners to look forward to.

With Pauline, however, hope springs eternal in her effort to snag a boyfriend. Pauline thinks to herself, "Well, I don't want someone who obviously doesn't want me. There's always Len, now. I might even be working with him one day with the San Xavier Police Department."

After completing her self-absorbed musing, Pauline says to Matt, "Well, I guess, I have all the self-confidence, I need, now. With your help, I solved, a substantial mystery, alas, not a murder, but a crime of corruption. I'm sure someone else with more taste than you will want me!"

Matt replied, genuinely amused, and dismayed at Pauline's

illusionary image of their relationship, "Pauline, let's not end this way. We can be friends. I can help your career. I have connections with the Postal Service, and the San Francisco Police Department. And I really and truly want to help you reach your goals. Can't we be friends?"

Fickle Pauline still liked Matt, although by this time in the conversation, she had fallen out of love with him. Alas, she realized, it was only "Puppy Love," as she hummed the song to herself, "And they called it "Puppy Love." The teenager of her youth, Donny Osmond, sang that top 100 hit pop song, "Puppy Love", way back in 1972, when she was an impressionable ten. Even though she finally recognized "Puppy Love", she still she did not want to burn her bridges behind her, so she simply said, "Okay. We'll write. I'll write you, and you can always write me."

"Pauline," Matt said, surprising himself with the wisdom of his own words, "Self-esteem is a choice. Self-worth is somewhat of a perplexity. It is a genuine mystery, but also a substantial illusion." Matt said this halfway, half as a question, half as a statement." Not something you acquire by accomplishments or just have, but an act of the will. What you have is illusionary; it can disappear, just like magic. You are a child of God, a little higher than the angels. That is what your genuine self-esteem should be based upon."

Pauline stared at him perplexed. Silently, incredulously, thinking, "This came out of flighty Matt?"

He continued, "Besides, think of all the practice, we had being quote boyfriend and girlfriend. You'll be ready for the genuine article, and so will I, if or when it comes along. This practice has been your epiphany. Your realization that you are worthy, not only because God created you, but … just because. Just because you believe in your intrinsic worth as a human being. Your truest identity derives from a relationship with a God who created you as an individual. Your true identity does not come from a career, and not from your so-called boyfriend."

Pauline looked up at Matt, so far unconvinced and still hurting from rejection, and said "What does that long winded, big bag of wind, stupid speech really mean? I'm so smart; you're so lucky to have met me?"

"Well, actually, yes, it does, and don't forget it means you practiced too," replied Matt smiling his Cheshire smile, once again.

Pauline flashed a halfway smile back at him, half amused, half friendly smile, which meant it was time to write you off, buster, but maybe we can still be friends, just to be friendly, and maybe to advance my career, along the way, kind of smile. And then there was a summer class coming up to distract her, and batting practice. Pauline's coach Sam had called her last night to tell her Marilyn Branson, the team's shortstop, had dropped off the team in order to spend more time with her inattentive police officer husband. The one who had his wallet stolen from the police car. Pauline was thinking about her upcoming new role as team shortstop later that evening during softball practice, when she said out loud to Matt, "Oh, yea, practice."

PLEASE REVIEW THE BOOK

If you have enjoyed this book, please share your opinions as a reviewer on the site where you purchased this book, and/or on the Goodreads website. If you believe the book is worth sharing please take a few minutes to share your opinions with others on your favorite social media site as well. In your review, I would like to know if you liked the book, and please feel free to leave me any advice for improving my next novella. Thank you.

 You just graduated from high school, or even college.

Do you need a superior how-to job hunting guide that can step-by-step easily train you on how-to write a winning resume, fabulous cover letter, and professional thank you note?

Do you need useful help? Yes you do.

Do you need super job hunting tips for the 21st century? Yes, you do!

You need *Super Man's Resume: A Beginner's Guide to Resume Writing and Beyond 2017 Edition* LS Wagen's job hunting, and resume writing guide.

Available in paperback and eBook format.

Order it today from www.amazon.com or from your favorite bookstore!!